D0448385

LOVE SUGAR
MAGIC
A SPRINKLE OF SPIRITS

ALSO BY ANNA MERIANO

Love Sugar Magic: A Dash of Trouble
Love Sugar Magic: A Mixture of Mischief

ANNA MERIANO

WALDEN POND PRESS
An Imprint of HarperCollins*Publishers*

When cooking, it is important to keep safety in mind. Children should always ask permission from an adult before cooking and should be supervised by an adult in the kitchen at all times. The publisher and author disclaim any liability from any injury that might result from the use, proper or improper, of the recipes contained in this book.

Walden Pond Press is an imprint of HarperCollins Publishers.
Walden Pond Press and the skipping stone logo are trademarks and registered trademarks of Walden Media, LLC.

Love Sugar Magic: A Sprinkle of Spirits
 For information address HarperCollins Children's Books, a division of HarperCollins Publishers, 195 Broadway, New York, NY 10007.
www.harpercollinschildrens.com

ISBN 978-0-06-249852-6

Typography by Sarah Nichole Kaufman
19 20 21 22 23 PC/BRR 10 9 8 7 6 5 4 3 2 1
❖
First paperback edition, 2020

To Mary Lou and Vince (Grandma and Grandpa) Meriano, thank you for your wisdom, humor, and unwavering support

LOVE SUGAR MAGIC
A SPRINKLE OF SPIRITS

CHAPTER 1

WELCOME BACK

"Leonora Elena Logroño, where did you disappear to?"

Leo jumped at the voice, glancing over her shoulder at the swinging blue doors that separated the kitchen from the front of the bakery, where she was, and her family's prying eyes from Leo's experiment.

Mamá was back!

"'Jita? We have luggage to unload, and I want a welcome-home hug!"

"She's out here, Mamá." Leo's sixteen-year-old sister, Marisol, peeked her head over the doors and smiled treacherously as she added, "Avoiding work."

"I am not," Leo yelped, hopping off the bakery

counter she wasn't supposed to sit on. "I was running the register like the schedule says." Leo grimaced. The bakery wouldn't open for another twenty minutes, but she wasn't quite as quick as her friend Caroline when it came to inventing excuses. Luckily, no one seemed to be listening.

Mamá's head joined Marisol's to peer into the front of the bakery. The large purple duffel bag over one shoulder and the smaller backpack on the other smacked the doors and sent them swinging open and shut. "Well?" she asked. "What about that hug?"

Leo smiled and rushed into the kitchen. "Welcome home," she said into her mother's shirt. "How was the convention?"

Mamá dumped her bags next to the long wooden table in the center of the kitchen, pushed strands of dark hair out of her face, and smiled. She had dressed for the early-morning road trip in jean shorts and a black T-shirt. "It was nice, 'jita."

Mamá and Isabel had spent the weekend at the Southwest Regional Brujería and Spellcraft Convention, the one time a year that brujos and brujas, witches and sorcerers from around Texas, Oklahoma, and Louisiana met up to swap stories and stock up on crow feathers and spider eggs and other components for spells. The SRBSC had a monthly newsletter too, but it almost always ended up unread in a pile on the Logroño kitchen table.

"Everything went perfectly while you were away," Leo said, puffing her chest out a little. Since school was still out for the rest of the week, she had been allowed to help at the bakery almost full-time. "We didn't even need you or Isabel to get ready for Día de los Reyes."

Amor y Azúcar Panadería smelled sweet and yeasty, two counters lined with trays of thick dough rings and the long wooden table scattered with dried fruit and bowls of sugar icing. Today was January 3, and that meant the next three days would be all about baking and selling rosca de reyes—kings' cake—to help the town of Rose Hill, Texas, celebrate Día de los Reyes.

"It does look good around here," Mamá said, nodding. "And it smells good!"

"Like Leo said." Marisol smirked. "We did just fine on our own."

"Well." Mamá stepped back and pretended to cover her injured heart. "Don't let me interfere with your preparations."

"We didn't mean it like that," Leo protested, hugging Mamá a second time in apology. "I'm glad you're back."

Mamá laughed. "Me too, 'jita. The holiday wouldn't be the same away from my family."

Three Kings' Day happened twelve days after Christmas, the day the wise men brought gifts to baby Jesus. There weren't as many movies about January 6 as there were about December 25, but Día de los Reyes always meant candy and cake and gifts left in kids' shoes overnight, and most important, parties with the people you loved.

"Did you see the new window display?" Leo asked her mother. "I did most of it. Well, and Marisol helped a little with the arranging."

Besides adding golden crowns and rosca de reyes into the bakery's front window, Leo's favorite part of the holiday was adding statues of the three kings—Balthazar with his dark skin, Gaspar with flat black painted hair, and Melchior, who looked like Dumbledore—to the nativity scene. About a week after Christmas, the family would set the statues in one corner of the window, and every day they would move them closer and closer to the manger.

"You would have been so proud of Leo," Tía Paloma said, bursting in through the back door of the bakery carrying two more of her sister's bags. "All the girls were a big help, which of course I expected, but Leo was especially focused this weekend. This whole break, really. We're all very proud of her progress."

Leo's smile bloomed and then wilted. Just this weekend? Wasn't she always focused? She studied her herb packets almost every day, so much that even her best friend, Caroline, could recite the uses of most of the basic bruja herbs.

"Except today, when she was supposed to be helping with the babies," Marisol muttered, leaning against the wall picking at her dark purple nail polish.

"I did help with them!" Leo made a face at Marisol. "I finished all the trays that were on the counter." All morning she had hidden tiny plastic babies in the dough of the cakes Tía Paloma lined up for baking. Rosca de reyes was special not just because of the cake's delicious sweet-bread taste or its colorful decoration, but also because of the baby figurine hidden inside. Whoever ate the slice of cake with the baby—which represented baby Jesus, born twelve days earlier—was in charge of making the tamales for the Día de la Candelaria party a few weeks later. Leo didn't know any other cakes that planned their own parties.

Before Marisol could say anything else snooty, Isabel walked in from the parking lot, her arms empty and her button-down shirt wrinkled from hours in the car. Leo ran to hug her oldest sister, who smoothed the top of Leo's hair and laughed.

"Hi, Little Leo. I was only gone for two days, you know."

"It felt longer," Leo protested.

"Only because you had to cover my shifts here," Isabel teased. Marisol snorted and muttered something rude, but Isabel ignored her. "It felt too short to me. There was so much to learn! Mamá barely let me talk to anyone, she was so busy using me as a pack mule for all the ingredients she bought."

This had been Isabel's first year to join Mamá at the convention. Going the whole weekend without her made Leo worry about next year, when Isabel would start college and move away, maybe even as far as San Antonio or Houston. Who would stand up to Marisol then? Still, it was exciting to think that someday she too could accompany Mamá and represent the bakery at the convention.

Isabel gestured at the bags, which Mamá and Tía Paloma had started opening to reveal jars of liquids and powders, bundles of herbs tied with string, and Ziploc bags full of everything from wooden beads to crystals to sand. Leo's fingers itched to touch everything, to sniff the packets for the telltale cinnamony smell of magic and ask what each ingredient was used for. She wanted to learn everything all at once, but Tía Paloma and Mamá wanted her to master the basics—which meant learning magic as slowly as bread dough rising. Leo had spent the last three months studying page after page of herb properties and running the cash register at the bakery, when what she really wanted to do was bake her own bona fide spells.

If Leo was honest, though, she did understand why Mamá and Tía Paloma wanted to take things slow. Three months ago, when Leo had first discovered her family's magic, she had tried to learn spells herself in secret, only to have her recipes make a mess so big, it took inventing a whole new spell just to clean it up. And if she was completely honest, she would admit that the rising time was an important part of the bread-making process. But none of that changed the impatient voice in her brain, whispering that she would never learn anything about magic if she didn't starting *doing* it.

Which was why she sometimes secretly entertained herself with . . . experiments. Nothing like her bungled love potions from last year. Just small magic charms. Like the one she'd been working on at the front counter that morning.

Isabel took charge of loading the ovens, while Mamá and Tía Paloma sorted the new magic ingredients into the tall cupboards along the far wall. Daddy poked his head out of the bakery office to welcome everyone home, but he quickly returned to his paperwork after Mamá shooed him away from sniffing a jar of dark powder. Leo had just started to shuffle toward the front of the bakery to continue her spell experiment when the bakery phone rang and two matching heads popped out from the office.

"Leo—" Alma said.

"—phone for you," Belén finished. The twins had celebrated their fifteenth birthday last month by dyeing the fading pink and blue stripes in their hair green and purple. You could tell the twins apart if you looked carefully, but most people didn't and just mixed up the two girls.

"Tell Caroline that we need that phone line for orders." Mamá sighed, guessing who was on the phone. "I've told you this before."

"Sorry," Leo said. Another day she might grumble at Mamá, or even argue that this was why she needed a cell phone of her own. But today she was happy to have her family all together, and she didn't want to argue.

Leo glanced at the blue swinging doors, anxious

about leaving her experiment out in the open, but nobody seemed to be in any rush to open the bakery. She walked back to the office, where Alma and Belén crowded Daddy out of most of his desk space with yellowed index cards spread everywhere. Belén held a stack of them, which she was sorting into different piles. She kept looking to the empty corner of the office, nodding and whispering questions as she went along.

If Leo hadn't known that there was an invisible person in the room holding the other side of the conversation, her sister would have looked pretty strange. But the twins, sharing the third-born spot in the family, had the special ability of seeing and talking to ghosts. Their winter-break project was consulting with Abuela, Bisabuela, and other ancestors from their mother's side of the family to decide which of their old family recipes were worth typing up to save in the bakery's computer system, and which could be retired and replaced.

Leo didn't have her special ability yet, or any special projects.

"Hello?" Leo took the phone from Daddy, who tapped her head with his pen and went back to his inventory lists.

"Hi, Leo!" Caroline Campbell, Leo's best friend

and sometimes coconspirator, chirped excitedly. "I'm back!" She had been gone for two whole weeks, visiting her grandmother and aunts in Costa Rica for Christmas and New Year's.

Leo laughed. "Join the club. My mom and Isabel just got back from their convention."

"You want to come over?" Caroline asked. "Later maybe? After you're done working? I have souvenirs."

Leo hesitated. Mamá probably had a family dinner planned to celebrate being back home from the convention. Leo really wanted to see Caroline, but she didn't want to miss any stories about other Texas brujas or different types of magic.

"Maybe . . . ," she started to say.

"What is this?" Marisol's voice rang out from the front of the bakery.

Leo closed her eyes. "Oh no . . ."

"Mamá!" Marisol yelled. "Leo's doing spells again!"

Alma and Belén looked up from their jumbled stacks of notecards, eyebrows lifted. Leo cringed. Of all the people she didn't want finding her experiment, Marisol was number one.

"Caroline, do me a favor? Wait five minutes and then call back?" With any luck Leo could use the phone call as an excuse to end the lecture she was about to get. She hung up the phone and scampered through the kitchen and into the front of the bakery.

Marisol, Mamá, Isabel, and Tía Paloma all stood around the counter, where a jar of honey and a tray of sticky plastic babies sat, the pieces of Leo's experiment.

"Leo, what's this?" Mamá asked.

"It looks like a mess," Marisol said, tilting the tray and watching the babies slide down the slant in slow motion, leaving sluglike honey trails. Isabel clicked her tongue at Marisol's rude comment, but she looked equally confused.

Leo's face felt like she was standing in front of an open oven door. "I wasn't going to do anything sneaky with it," she promised. "I would have shown you as soon as I finished." She stuck her tongue out at Marisol.

"Good," Mamá said. "Why don't you go ahead and show me now?"

Leo squinted at her mother. Was she hiding her anger behind curiosity? Or did she really want to know? All she could see in Mamá's face were tired lines from a long weekend.

"You're initiated," Mamá reminded her. "You're not going to get in trouble for some little spell.

However, we don't want any more unsupervised fiascos. Just be honest, 'jita."

Isabel leaned over the tray for a closer look. "I can feel some magic in them," she said. "What were you trying, Little Leo?"

Leo tried not to roll her eyes at the babyish nickname. She tried to remember that she had been officially initiated into the family magic even after Mamá caught her messing with magic last November, before she was allowed to. That she was a bruja, just like her older sisters.

"It was going to be a prosperity charm," she explained, lifting the honey jar and shaking it to show them the clinking quarters at the bottom. "I thought whoever got the baby could use a little help paying for a whole party's worth of tamales."

Mamá reached for the sticky jar and sniffed it. "Not a bad idea," she said slowly, "but a little messy. It might make the babies sink in the dough, too. Why not put the spell on the dolls without the honey?"

"They're made of plastic." Tía Paloma spoke up, her head cocked to one side. "Not a good conductor, even in human shape, which of course will strengthen it, but . . . right." She nodded, either forgetting to speak her thoughts aloud or listening to a ghost—it was hard to tell with Tía Paloma, who tended to live in her own world, just like the twins. "I think getting some sugar in there is smart for a beginner."

Leo nodded. The magic of her mother's family was the magic they had named their bakery after: Amor y Azúcar. Love and Sugar. Anything sweet and delicious held their magic easily, which was why the magical recipes they saved in the family spell book all included ingredients like sugar or flour (which broke down to make sugar). Leo studied the magical properties of herbs and plants with her Tía Paloma most afternoons, but she had never tried to work a spell that didn't involve sugar.

Tía Paloma and Mamá stared at the honey, both of their mouths twisted in thought. The heat in Leo's face crept into her ears, but now it was warm pride that her silly experiment was being considered like a real spell. Maybe this would be her first entry into the spell book. Maybe she was a magical prodigy. Maybe . . .

"Leo!" Belén poked her head through the swinging doors. And held out the bakery phone. "Your friend is on the phone again."

Had it been five minutes already? Leo took the phone from her sister. "Hi, Caroline . . . sorry, I'm actually sort of—"

"It's fine," Caroline said. "I just really wanted to tell you about my trip."

"If the dolls were made of wax," Isabel was saying, "they'd hold the spell pretty well, I bet."

"Yeah, but they'd also melt as soon as they went in the oven," Marisol said, rolling her eyes.

Caroline was still talking, but Leo leaned toward her family. She didn't know wax held magic better than plastic. She wanted to hear about Caroline's trip, but she didn't want to miss learning anything about magic—especially when it was about a spell she had created!

"Oh, Paloma! You should start the little girls on candle work," Mamá said. "Alma and Belén will need to know more about using candles for summoning, and Leo's curiosity is a lot less messy when it's satisfied." She winked at Leo, who smiled back and let the phone drop from her ear.

"After Dia de los Reyes?" Tía Paloma asked.

"Why wait?" Mamá asked. "I've missed my kitchen, and with the rosca de reyes lined up, we'll be fine here until noon at least. Take them to your house and get them out of my hair for a little bit."

"Hello? Can you hear me?" Caroline said.

Leo put the phone back up to her ear, feeling guilty. "Yes, I'm here," she said.

"Stupid reception." Caroline sighed. "So do you think you can come over? I have *so* much to tell you. I missed you!"

"I . . ."

Tía Paloma clapped her hands and called for Alma to leave the office. "Come on, Leo! Magic lesson at my house. Tell Caroline you'll talk to her later."

"That's why she's been focused lately," Marisol said. "Caroline has been out of town."

"That's right." Isabel nodded. "I noticed she wasn't as distracted, but I thought it was just because we didn't have school."

If Leo's brain weren't being stretched in ten different directions, she could have told Marisol and Isabel that Caroline wasn't a distraction, thank you very much. Caroline did stop by the bakery after school almost every day, but most of the time she was helping Leo study the new herbs on her list or helping her brainstorm cool ideas for spells. But Belén tugged on Leo's sleeve, and Tía Paloma's smile held the promise of new magic, and Leo didn't want to be distracted or left behind.

"I'm sorry, I have to go," she told Caroline. "I have to work."

"Maybe I can stop by later on?" Caroline said.

"Yeah, maybe." Leo frowned at Isabel and Marisol,

even though they weren't looking at her. "I have to go, okay? Bye."

She hung up the phone and left it on the counter next to her prosperity honey.

"Wait for me!" She raced into the kitchen in time to see Tía Paloma and the twins disappear out the back door. "I'm coming!"

CHAPTER 2

CANDLE MAGIC

January rain dripped from the gray sky as they left the bakery. Tía Paloma lived in Abuela's old house, not far from the bakery. But Leo's aunt drove the way she talked, weaving back and forth between lanes, taking wrong turns and confusing shortcuts. By the time they pulled up to the sagging front porch of the boxy wooden house, Leo was sure they'd circled all of Rose Hill, twice.

"All right, come in, come in." Tía Paloma ushered Leo and her sisters through the front door. The house was narrow and tall, with a high, pointed roof and wooden boards for walls instead of the brick that made up most of Leo's neighborhood. The corners of every room were filled with boxes, piles of papers and books, and mysterious knickknacks collected by generations of bakery brujas. Leo loved to inspect them whenever she visited—stone statues with too many legs, wooden paintings of saints that unfolded like books, strings of tiny seed beads on colorful thread, thin rusty keys hidden in drawers. Even before she had known about the family magic, Leo had always suspected that Tía Paloma lived with ghosts.

Alma and Belén headed immediately for the dining-room table. They had taken special lessons with their aunt since their powers came and they were first able to see ghosts, so they were used to coming here to learn. Leo, on the other hand, got all her magic instruction shouted over the whir of the electric mixers and the beep of the oven timers in the bakery kitchen.

Tía Paloma waved a hand to stop the twins before they sat down. "No, not there, not today. I'm showing you the *candle room* today. I want to demonstrate how to use them in spells beyond just the ones I've shown you. We haven't really discussed . . . what?" She turned her head to the back of the room, and Alma and Belén followed her gaze. "Yes, I did.

Well, they know. Well then, I'm about to tell her, if you'll let me—" Tía Paloma sighed and tossed her ponytail, ending the conversation with Abuela, or whoever she was talking to, much to Leo's relief. It was hard being the only person in the room who couldn't hear ghosts.

"Just follow me, girls," Tía Paloma said. "This is something new."

Leo shivered and bounced on her toes. She wanted to know every place the magic hid. She followed her aunt and sisters through the large kitchen, the faded fruit pattern of the wallpaper as familiar as the collage of photographs on the fridge that showed the women and girls of Leo's family smiling in the same kitchen, in front of mixing bowls or trays of perfectly iced cookies or cakes. Whether the photos were old, faded Polaroids of Abuela and her three daughters or newly printed digital snapshots of Alma and Leo filling pies for Thanksgiving, they all contained the same hanging rack of copper pots and pans, the same white-and-blue butter churn that was inexplicably filled with so many pennies and nickles and dimes that it couldn't be budged from its spot next to the counter.

Just like she did every time she passed the fridge, Tía Paloma brushed her fingers across the photo in the center, which showed little-kid Mamá, toddler Tía Paloma, and a taller third girl with short messy pigtails and a mischievous smile. Tía Paloma cried in the picture, her hand reaching for a cookie held just out of reach by her smirking sister.

Leo's oldest aunt had died in an accident when Mamá and Tía Paloma were still young, and even though Leo knew her sister Isabel shared her name and her first-born power to influence people's emotions, all the stories Mamá and Tía Paloma told about their eldest sister made her sound more like Marisol—a troublemaker.

They continued down the cramped hallway, past Tía Paloma's old bedroom, now full of craft supplies and half-finished projects of all kinds; past Mamá's old bedroom, now a cluttered guest room. Leo had once found an old collection of polished stones in the boxes under the bed, and Tía Paloma had let her keep her favorite one. Leo had been sure the shiny silvery-black rock was magic, but now she knew that Tía Paloma didn't give magic objects to little kids. She kept them in special cupboards and bookshelves—and, apparently, candle rooms.

Two doors stood at the end of the hall. One was Tía Paloma's master bedroom, where her pair of orange cats always lurked to avoid the noisy Logroños, and the other was the only room in the house Leo had never seen before: Tía Isabel's old bedroom.

The door was covered in black-and-neon stickers, with bundles of herbs taped in each corner and charts of moon phases overlapping posters of angry-looking musicians and photos and drawings of Day of the Dead ofrendas, glowing orange with marigold flowers and candle flames. Leo wondered if Mamá's door had once been decorated to show her personality, and what it would have looked like. Did she love magic like her older sister? Did she listen to bands that wore black and raised their fists at the camera? Would Tía Isabel have taken all her decorations down if she had lived to be older?

Tía Paloma stopped in front of the messy door, took a breath, and knocked.

Leo tensed her shoulders, expecting something ghostly to happen. Alma and Belén looked around the hallway and cocked their heads, but then Alma caught Leo's eye and shrugged.

"I always check for Isabel, just in case." Tía Paloma sighed, shook her head, and opened the door.

Alma and Belén gasped in stereo on either side of Leo. She had imagined that the room, like the door, would be frozen exactly the way Tía Isabel had left it, but there was no bed or any bedroom furniture.

It looked more like Tía Paloma's craft room, with the same easy-assembly plastic shelves filling in the spaces between more antique wooden shelves that leaned against the walls like they might collapse into a pile of dust and splinters at any moment. There was plenty of work space in the form of long wooden tables lined up across the room, the dark wood of the legs carved into familiar shapes and patterns, and Leo smiled when she recognized them. The tables matched the tall cabinets in the bakery, the ones that held ingredients both commonplace and magical. Both the shiny plastic and the weathered wood glowed in the dim light of the room.

Candles flickered in each shelf cubby, their flames dotting the dark room with eerie blue light instead of normal orange fire. One table held jars of powders stacked in rows with neat labels, and another drew her eye with bundles of herbs, folded papers, and a box of matches lying in a pool of bright yellow-orange light from a few candles lit the normal way. It looked almost like an ofrenda from Día de los Muertos, but Leo guessed that this candle cluster stayed up all year round, not just in November. An altar.

Although the candles were all the way across the room, the warmth of tiny flames prickled Leo's face and danced in her stomach.

"Beautiful," Alma whispered in Leo's ear.

Belén giggled and reached around Leo to poke Alma's shoulder. "Isn't it kind of a fire hazard, though?"

Tía Paloma flicked a light switch. In the glare of the overhead lamp, all the blue flames disappeared, leaving a smoky odor and hints of other scents both strange and familiar, and only the small group of candles in the center of the room still burned. Leo walked to the cluster and examined a tiny nub of a pink candle, burning at the bottom of a tall glass.

"I lit that one for your mamá," Tía Paloma said, pushing the candle away from Leo's outstretched hand. "I thought she would need all the communication help she could get at the conference. You know, in a small community like ours, everybody talks. I'm sure you and your . . . accidents were a topic of conversation, Leo."

Leo hung her head. Her attempts to learn magic on her own in November had shrunk a boy and attracted the attention of the police, so of course the other magic workers would know about them. It was scary to think of a bunch of adult spell casters shaking their heads and talking about the out-of-control Logroño bruja. Leo didn't want to make Mamá look bad.

But now she was initiated, and she was learning

magic the right way, and the next time the spell-casting convention met, they would be talking about Leo with pride.

"So," Leo said, eager to get started, "candles can help when you're trying to talk to other people?"

"That's one of the uses of the pink ones," Tía Paloma said. "But I'm getting ahead of myself. Your mother and I want to make sure you get a rounded education, you know, in spell work. And, well, candles and herbs are so important. I'm sure your mamá feels this, especially after spending a weekend in the larger community—working with your aptitude, your own special ability, is wonderful, but we can't ignore the tools and traditions that connect us all. That's why we have the convention, isn't it? So this is the candle room, where we can prepare and light candles for anything we . . ." She fell quiet for a moment, as if lost in thought. "Oh, and you girls can use them, of course, if you ever need to; they're not just mine. They're for the family."

Leo tilted her head, not sure if it would be rude to tell Tía Paloma that she was making even less sense than usual.

"Right." Tía Paloma nodded toward the corner of the room. "Of course, that's not to say you should go running off to tell everyone you know."

Alma and Belén both turned to look at Leo with raised eyebrows.

Leo rolled her eyes. "I'm not going to." She realized what the twins must be thinking and looked down. "Caroline isn't *everyone*."

"Oh, goodness." Tía Paloma sighed. "I should have lit one of these for myself before I started trying to explain all of this to you! I didn't mean to single you out, Leo. And your friend has always seemed trustworthy." She frowned as she lifted the glass with the pink candle, inspected it, then covered the top of the glass until the small flame shrank and died.

Leo bit her lip, trying to push down her annoyance. She didn't want to worry about her family's disapproval of Caroline right now. She wanted to learn magic.

As if she could read Leo's thoughts, Tía Paloma clapped her hands and waved them in a sweeping circle around the room. "Veladoras," she said, "come in all shapes and sizes. Just like the herbs we've been learning about, each type of candle has specific properties, and once you've learned them, they can be components of larger spells."

"Like when we summon spirits to speak to the living," Alma said with a nod. Leo remembered when the twins had used a candle to make her abuela appear as a ghost in the middle of Leo's bedroom.

"But that's our special birth-order power," Belén said. "Isabel or Leo can't light a candle and talk to ghosts, can they?"

Tía Paloma riffled through one of the shelves. "Well, no one really knows what Leo can or can't do, since we've never had a fourth-born before. But you're right; your sisters can't use candles the same way you can. Here, hold this."

She pulled a tall, skinny brown candle off the shelf and passed it to Belén. The candle was stuck like a straw through a cardboard circle, making it look like a sword when Belén wrapped her hand around the bottom third. Tía Paloma picked up a match from the altar and lit the candle. She squinted at it for a moment before grabbing Leo and Alma each by a shoulder and pushing them close around Belén like they were squeezing in for a selfie.

Leo looked at the twins and they looked back at Leo, eyebrows raised past their colored bangs in mirrored confusion. Leo guessed Tía Paloma was trying to work a spell with the brown candle, casting something on the three girls.

"Rosemary!" Tía Paloma gasped suddenly. "That would kick this up from a suggestion to a real spell. I know I have some around somewhere—it's used for concentration, you know, which is why I find it handy to keep around. Helps me stay a little more . . ." She tilted her head at Leo, who quickly tried to make her face look less like a gaping fish. ". . . focused. I'm confusing you, aren't I?"

Leo shrugged, even though the answer was yes.

"Magic comes in many forms, but for our lessons it helps to break magic into two categories: aptitudes and relics. Aptitudes are inherent magical abilities, like our family's affinity for sugar and flour, and our birth-order powers. Even if you had no magical materials handy, any of you girls could cook up a powerful recipe or spell on your own."

Leo nodded. Isabel had shown her a spell she could do with just a palmful of flour once.

"Relics are objects that carry power within them. Herbs or candles, crystals or religious symbols or chants, even certain foods can be relics, though usually weak ones." Tía Paloma spread her hands toward the candles all around the room. "Someone with almost no aptitude could use a candle to channel magic into their life, just like someone with no talent for baking can still follow a recipe and end up with something mostly edible."

Thanks to her lunchtime snack club, Leo had tasted plenty of cookies and cakes baked by her friends with no baking experience. They tasted all right, but they didn't carry the same power as Mamá's baked goods—the power to put a smile on the face of anyone who ate them.

"So candles can help with baking magic," Leo said slowly, "but baking magic doesn't really need candles?" It sounded like one of the logic puzzles her teacher, Ms. Wood, gave out as extra credit for math sometimes.

"But we use candles to summon spirits," Belén said thoughtfully, her eyes glued to the flickering flames of her brown candle. "Does that mean everyone can do that?"

"No, no." Tía Paloma shook her head. She scooted aside the candles on the table, picking a fat purple candle off a shelf and sprinkling a pinch of powder over the top of it before lighting it. "Relics on their own have broad uses but are more subtle in their effects, opening paths and adding flavor to other magical forces. Aptitude on its own can be flashy, but is usually quite narrow, like how our abilities with spirits are limited to seeing and hearing them." The light of the candle wavered as Tía Paloma passed her hand through the flame, her fingers casting long shadows that rippled into a rainbow of dark colors and starbursts across the ceiling. Alma yelped,

Belén whistled, and Leo opened her mouth in awe.

"When you combine aptitude with relics, then you can really do amazing things. That's how our family creates our most complex recipes, and it's why I want you girls to know the uses of herbs and candles. It can help you all do more with your magic."

Leo felt something bubble in her chest as Tía Paloma's words finally clicked together to make sense in her head. She wanted to do more with her magic. She wanted to use everything she could to help her channel her powers.

She wanted to learn *everything.*

"So how do we start?" she asked.

CHAPTER 3

CAROLINE CRASHES

Leo had woken up every day of vacation feeling extra lucky to have more time to spend at the bakery. Even though it meant leaving the house with Mamá and her sisters at five a.m., Leo loved watching the shop lights flicker on, feeling the ovens heat up, and smelling the first batches of conchas and bolillos as they turned golden brown. More time with her family also meant more chances to pick up magic tips; even when no one was purposely teaching her, Leo could listen and learn. Sometimes she even got to help Isabel gather rare ingredients for one of the bakery's special magical orders. Leo couldn't wait for the day when Mamá would trust her to bake someone's lucky birthday cake herself.

The morning after the candle lesson, January 4, started extra early. There were trays of rosca de reyes to bake and box, shelves to fill, and all sorts of dough to make, from pastry to cookie to biscuit. Leo skipped into the bakery behind her line of sleepy sisters, pulling one of the Amor y Azúcar aprons out of the clean laundry bag and slipping it over her braided hair.

Tía Paloma arrived twenty minutes late with a huge tote bag full of candles and a thin book with yellowed edges and a crumbling cover. "I made copies," she said, passing Leo a neat paper clipped packet with grainy gray images of tattered paper with scratchy handwriting.

Leo grabbed her pages with delight. There were illustrations of different types of candles, drawn by a shaky hand, next to a chart that listed various uses for all different colors. Though the book was in Spanish, Leo recognized some of the information that Tía Paloma had gone over the day before: pink for smoothing relationships, brown for clearing minds, plain yellow to connect to the spirit world, purple for creating illusions. It felt like figuring out how variables worked in pre-algebra. A few months ago, Leo had barely discovered that magic existed, and now there were a thousand new ways to use it.

Leo set the packet down as her family yawned through their opening morning routine. Mamá and Tía Paloma moved around the kitchen like matching whirlwinds, filling mixing bowls with flour and freeing cartons of eggs from the walk-in refrigerator. Leo helped Alma and Belén unload yesterday's dishes from the dishwasher while Isabel flipped on the grumbling air conditioner and wiped down all the display cases and shelves. The glow of the ovens matched the glow of the sunrise through the windows. Marisol finished the morning's first pot of coffee and set the machine to brew a second before Mamá could catch her downing her cup.

The sun lit up the sky and the oven timers pinged steadily when Daddy's pickup truck pulled into the parking lot. He always said that he was lucky that invoices and receipts, unlike bread, could wait an hour or two when he felt like sleeping in.

Her morning work finished, Leo nibbled on a day-old concha and listened to Alma and Belén argue about who had stolen whose favorite shirt first. She wondered if there was a spell to stop a thief, and what sort of candles or herbs it would use.

"Leonora," Daddy called from the office. "There's a message here for you from yesterday."

Leo winced. She had been so excited thinking about the lesson last night, she hadn't remembered to call Caroline.

"Actually, there are messages. Plural."

Alma exchanged an eye roll with Belén, and Leo's heart sank. Her sisters' disapproval always made her feel about two inches tall.

"I'll listen later," she said loudly. "I want to study right now." She shouldn't have to prove that she was serious about magic, but she snatched Tía Paloma's candle packet and clutched it to her chest. Caroline probably wasn't awake yet, anyway.

She stomped to the front counter, knowing without having to check that the whiteboard schedule in the office had her listed once again on cashier duty. She had planned to beg her way into helping Isabel with the decorations on the first few batches of rosca de reyes, but now she perched grumpily on a stool and focused on decoding the copied book.

The charts were simple enough to follow and the illustrations helped, but the twisty cursive and Spanish words made Leo's work slow. Tía Paloma often forgot that Leo had never talked with her abuela much before she died and couldn't speak Spanish fluently like her older sisters. That was another thing Caroline helped her with. Unlike Leo, Caroline could read and understand Spanish almost perfectly, and only struggled a little with her speaking. That was another reason why having Caroline help her study her magic lessons should be a good thing, not something her sisters rolled their eyes at.

Leo flipped through the packet to find the clearest passages while the first round of morning traffic whizzed past the windows and Isabel filled the shelves around her with fresh pan dulce. She was so absorbed that she didn't notice the ringing bell or the swish of the front door as the morning's first customer entered the shop.

"Leo?" The voice startled Leo into dropping her packet, pages escaping their paper clip and falling into a jumble on the floor.

"Caroline!" Leo slid down from the counter and bent to collect the scattered packet. "What are you doing here?"

"I didn't hear from you." Caroline stayed in the doorway with an uncertain expression, her fingers pulling the edges of her purple sweater together. "So I just thought I could walk over and see . . ."

Leo ran to hug her friend, the pages of her photocopied stack dropping, out of order, across the counter. "How was Costa Rica? How is your grandmother? How did you get your dad to let you walk here alone?"

No matter what her family said, Leo didn't feel like Caroline was a distraction to her focus. She was Leo's friend, and having her around made everything better. Like, for example, reading dense Spanish passages about candle magic.

Caroline's face relaxed into a smile when Leo let her go. "Thanks, it was good. I mean, it was okay." She pushed the hood of her sweater off her head.

"Do you want a cinnamon roll?" Leo offered. Maybe if she filled Caroline's stomach, then the guilt gnawing at her stomach would subside.

"I already ate Toaster Strudel," Caroline said. "I knew you'd be here at five, and so I got up early, hoping . . . you might call."

Guilt dug its teeth deeper into Leo's gut. "Have one," she pleaded. She felt very relieved when her friend smiled and nodded. Once Leo explained about the candle magic, Caroline would understand. It was hard to remember normal things when there were so many magical things to learn.

Caroline used a pair of hanging tongs to pull one of the flaky cinnamon rolls from its shelf. The dry rolls weren't as delicious as the gooey ones Leo sometimes made at home, but they were easier for customers to pick up.

"Thanks," Caroline said. "My dad walked me to

Main Street. His parenting books say that now is a good time for me to start *asserting my independence in safe contexts*, so he let me walk here while he went to the hardware store. The bad news is he's picking paint colors, so I'm probably going to get stuck repainting another room this weekend."

Leo nodded. Ever since Caroline's mother had died, not quite one year ago, Mr. Campbell had been remodeling, rearranging, and repainting their house. He was becoming a pretty good interior designer, but Caroline swore all the paint fumes were going to stunt her growth. Since her blond ponytail already bobbed a few inches above Leo's head, Leo thought she could maybe afford to be stunted, just a little.

"Want to see something cool?" Leo asked, shuffling her papers into a neater stack and holding them up as Caroline brought her cinnamon roll behind the counter. "Tía Paloma is teaching me a whole new type of magic. No more leaf shapes to memorize."

"Oh." Caroline peeled bite-size pieces off the edge of her pastry. "I liked learning the herbs. But this is something different?"

"Yeah, it's so cool." Leo grinned. "It's all candles, how they can change the energy of a situation and how they can strengthen certain types of spells. I'm learning about types of candles—or, um, veladora, I guess . . ."

"Or velas." Caroline shrugged. "Either one."

"Right—we're learning which kind to use and what you can do with them. And that's why I didn't call last night. Tía Paloma was teaching us and I got distracted. Sorry."

Caroline rolled bits of cinnamon filling into balls and popped them into her mouth. "Yeah . . . ," she said. "I get it. Casting spells with candles is a lot more exciting than getting lost in Costa Rica."

"You got lost?" Leo asked. "How? Where?"

Caroline's face relaxed, and she looked up from her cinnamon roll with a sheepish smile. "In the airport. Everyone thought we were tourists. I mean, we basically were." She sighed. "It was . . . weird. Going without my mom. It felt different."

Caroline had moved away to Houston for her mom's treatment, so Leo had lost contact with her friend during the worst part of Mrs. Campbell's illness and death. Even when Caroline and her dad moved back to Rose Hill, her next-door neighbor Brent had been the one to help lift the dark cloud and cheer Caroline up enough to come back to school. She would sometimes mention her mom, but she had never talked to Leo about the pain of losing her. Leo hadn't even realized that this was

Caroline's first time visiting Costa Rica without her mother.

"I'm sorry," she said. "That sounds so—"

"It was like I didn't—" Caroline started to say.

The swinging creak of the blue doors made both girls jump.

"Leo," Isabel said, pushing the door with her shoulder and walking backward through it, a tray of fresh conchas balanced on her arm. "Mamá says if there are no customers, you can get started gathering supplies for special orders. We have to make ocean breeze conchas for relaxation, and she wants me and Marisol to get the dough started for the listening orejas—" She turned around carefully and stopped. "Oh. Caroline. Good morning. Um." Isabel shifted from one foot to the other, the conchas wobbling dangerously on the tray. "Well, we'll talk later, Leo." She walked briskly to add the conchas to the earlier batches already on the shelves, sliding the pan dulce off the tray and turning them so they sat right side up and attractive.

Caroline ducked her head so that her eyes hid behind her bangs.

Leo jutted out her lower jaw in frustration. Why did Isabel have to act like Caroline was some stranger who couldn't hear about magic? Caroline had been Leo's partner in crime when she did her first disastrous spells in November. Caroline already knew they were brujas, so Leo didn't understand what her sister was acting so squirrely for. It made Leo mad to see Caroline hunch her shoulders and shift from one foot to the other, nibbling on her thumbnail.

She just wasn't sure if it was Isabel she was mad at, or herself for not saying anything.

"Well, I should go anyway," Caroline said.

"No, wait—"

"I didn't mean to make you—" Isabel's words tripped over Leo's.

"You didn't. I shouldn't have come while you were all still opening the bakery. I'm in your way. I don't . . ." Caroline took a deep breath. "I don't belong here, either."

She took a few steps to the trash can at the end of the counter. As she dropped her cinnamon roll with a clang and spun on her heel, she crashed straight into Belén, who barreled through the blue doors with an armful of veladoras.

Caroline screeched. Belén saved most of her cargo by flailing her arms like a juggler and falling to the ground to catch some candles in her lap, but two thick purple candles dented their edges toppling onto the tile floor, and one skinny pink one encased in glass hit the edge of the counter and shattered.

Belén said some words that made Mamá shout her name from the kitchen. Caroline knelt to help gather the glass shards but was quickly shooed away by Isabel. Belén passed the candles to Leo and Caroline, who lined them up on the counter as she swept the mess into the dustpan Alma brought her.

"I'm sorry," Leo whispered to Caroline. "My sisters are . . . they're just weird. They didn't mean to be—"

"Leo." Mamá walked into the front of the shop, her worried eyes quickly scanning the scene before turning stormy mad. "What are you doing, 'jita? You were supposed to be helping, or studying, not making messes. You know we're busy this week. Where is your head?" She stared down at Leo, wearing her most disappointed expression.

"I didn't make any messes," Leo protested. "Caroline was the one who—"

She clapped her hand over her mouth, but it was too late. She saw the hurt in Caroline's eyes turn liquid and spill over her eyelashes. Her friend shoved her hands into her sweater pockets, shook her head hard, and then turned and marched out of the bakery without saying a word.

CHAPTER 4

CHOICES

"What's her problem?" Belén asked, emptying the dustpan and handing it back to Alma.

Mamá patted Leo's shoulder, her frown disappearing as she watched Caroline leave. "Sorry, 'jita, I thought . . . well. Maybe I'm a little tired from the trip still. I know you're helping. I don't really mind having Caroline around."

"But does she always have to be around? Calling the bakery phone, and showing up like that?" Isabel asked. "This is a business, not a playground. And not just any business." Her eyes darted toward the front door to make sure no more customers were coming in. "You know, at the convention we discussed the *necessary precautions of discretion in an increasingly polarized world.*"

Whenever Isabel used that tone of voice, it meant she was discussing *very important grown-up issues.* Leo rolled her eyes.

"Caroline already knows about magic," she reminded Isabel, turning to Mamá for support, "and some people have to know we do magic—who would know to ask for all those special orders, if no one who wasn't a bruja knew about us? It's not like it's some big secret, right?"

"Well." Mamá sighed. "It's a little bit complicated. Some of our best customers here in Rose Hill know something about what we do, but we're certainly not advertising our spells far and wide, and I think it's best to keep it that way. This sounds like a topic for a family meeting, some time when we're not all upset and busy with—"

The beeping of an oven interrupted her, and she patted Leo's hair as she rushed toward the back of the kitchen. "We'll talk," she promised, "as soon as we can all have a breather!" She hurried back into the kitchen.

Leo balled her fists and ground the toe of her sneaker against a spiderweb crack in the tile.

Belén sighed and shrugged. She had gathered up her armful of candles. "Tía Paloma told me not to light any more of these inside, so we're heading to the parking lot to test out some potential spell ideas."

"We were going to try to see if the right type of candle can help us channel without using so much power," Alma added. "Do you want to come, Leo? You could try lighting a pink candle to help make up with Caroline."

Leo felt like a rubber band pulled from too many sides. She wanted to join the twins in the parking lot and see if she could pick up some interesting tricks from their new magic lessons. She wanted to run out the front door and chase Caroline down to apologize. She wanted to stay here and show Mamá that she *was* focused, that she was helping.

"Maybe I'll meet you out there."

"Sure." Alma waved with one hand while grabbing a teetering candle before it fell out of Belén's grasp. "Oh no, where did the yellow one go? Did you drop it? I rolled it in some crushed-up Solomon's seal to see if that would add strength, and I really wanted to see how that worked. . . ." The twins headed through the doors, bickering softly about candles and herbs.

Leo whirled angrily to face Isabel. "Why did you do that?"

"Do what?" Isabel asked, standing and brushing her knees as she finished inspecting the floor for shards. She picked up the empty conchas tray and held it in front of her stomach like a shield.

"Caroline helps me study. She's seen the spell book. You don't have be so rude; she knows about magic, and she's always been trustworthy."

Isabel sighed, lowering the tray to the floor. "Oh, Leo, I know that."

"Then why are you so weird about it?" Leo's stomach ached remembering Caroline's sad face, and it felt good to blame Isabel and her family and all their confusing rules. She thought of the Día de los Muertos festival, how she had snuck into the tent where Alma and Belén were secretly helping people contact their loved ones who had passed on. "Why do only some people get to know about what we do? Like Alma and Belén's messenger booth at the festival? I mean, I didn't even know what the booth was for until I decided to spy on them!"

"It's like Mamá said. Complicated."

Leo threw up her hands. "Complicated" was what everyone said when they didn't have any good reasons and didn't want to explain themselves.

"This is why we usually wait until everyone is fifteen to initiate—" Isabel started, but she pressed her lips together when she saw Leo's face turn dark.

This again. She had thought that being initiated into the family magic, getting permission to study and work in the bakery, would put an end to her sisters holding her age against her, but they still reminded her that she wasn't old enough or smart enough. "I don't care that I'm not fifteen. I don't care if you think I'm too young." Leo spat the lie like sour milk to get the taste out of her mouth. She felt ready to scream.

"If you would just calm down for a second . . ." Isabel took a deep breath. As she let it out, a soft feeling settled over Leo's skin, raising goose bumps on her arms. Her head felt light, and the sharp bite of guilt and resentment started to loosen its hold on her stomach. Annoyance bloomed underneath the calm as she realized that Isabel was using her special power of influence to soothe Leo's emotions, but soon even that pain melted away into stillness.

"Stop it," Leo said. Her voice was soft in her ears. If she was Marisol, she would roughen it into a hiss, push back against Isabel's spell, and get even madder than before, just to prove she could.

Isabel dropped the spell. Leo's head steadied

and her skin prickled again. Her troubled feelings returned in a wave of tension, but she felt them less fiercely than before. She didn't mind Isabel's power. It was helpful to quiet her mind so she could focus on her question.

"I guess I just don't understand. How secret is our magic supposed to be?" Leo asked.

"It's not exactly secret," Isabel said. "We're registered for the Southwest Regional Brujería and Spellcraft newsletter; it's not like we're in hiding. It's just . . . people who aren't brujas . . . they don't always understand. Our customers who know are the people we trust to keep quiet, and not to spread lies or mistrust about what we do. I'm sure you know that some people think brujos and brujas do evil magic. We can't take the risk of one of those people finding out about us."

Leo nodded. It was beginning to make sense, now that Isabel was actually explaining it. She imagined what would happen if her friend Brent's mom, who loved to gossip and complain, found out Leo had accidentally shrunk her son in November. She would do everything she could to put the bakery out of business, and probably to get Leo arrested!

"I know Caroline is your friend," Isabel continued, "but she's already used you to magically solve her problems once. The more she knows about your powers—"

"That wasn't Caroline's idea," Leo interrupted. When she had cast the love spells that went so wrong, it was Caroline who had tried to convince *her* to be more careful. "And even if she did, so what? Lots of people need magic help. That's why we have this bakery in the first place."

"Customers are different. Most of them just think we make ordinary—but extraordinarily delicious—breads and cakes." She smiled. "The rest, who know what we do, pay for an answer, or a feeling, or a superstition. Half the time they don't really believe in what they're buying. Or they don't know how everything works, they just know that it does. They don't really understand our powers. It's easier that way. They don't get scared, or angry, or ask for more than we can deliver."

Leo shrugged. It didn't sound easier to her. Wouldn't everyone rather have a friend like Caroline, who helped her learn about her power, than customers who used it without caring where it came from?

"I'm just saying," Isabel said. "Sometimes you have to choose, Leo. It's good to have friends at school, but they're never going to be like your family, and they're never going to understand . . . all of this."

Choose? Leo didn't want to choose between Caroline and her sisters. She wanted her family to include Caroline so she didn't have to choose.

"Isabel, why is it that every time I turn around, you're telling Leo something horrible?" Marisol emerged from the kitchen with her own tray of pastries, which she immediately passed off to Isabel so she could lounge against the wall and raise an eyebrow at Leo. "Always consider the source, cucaracha. Isabel thinks nobody can have friends just because *she* doesn't have any."

Isabel clattered the sweet queso-filled buns onto the shelf with a huff, but she didn't exactly deny what Marisol said.

"If you're obsessed with memorizing Tía Paloma's lists"—Marisol nodded at Leo's stack of papers on the counter—"and staying here until midnight making lucky bread, then of course you're not going to have good friends. But that's your decision. You can go after Caroline right now if it matters to you. Blow off the schedule, make up with your friend. Or you can stay here and compete with Isabel to be the world's most powerful and lonely bruja." Marisol snatched a cuervo off the shelf and took a bite. "Up to you."

Leo looked from Marisol to Isabel, annoyance again rushing up into her cheeks. Her two eldest sisters—who never agreed on anything—were too busy glaring at each other to realize that they were telling her the same exact thing: choose.

Between magic and friendship?

Leo didn't want to give up either one. But . . . did Mamá have friends? Leo frowned. Mamá was closest to Tía Paloma, and she had friends from the brujería convention. Friends who had their own magic. And Tía Paloma didn't have many *living* friends, but she was Tía Paloma.

Leo stomped past both her older sisters, gathered up her papers, and crossed through the kitchen to join Alma and Belén in the parking lot. The twins consulted with each other (and possibly with more ghostly observers) in whispers, crouched around a pink candle—for communication—that Alma rolled carefully up and down a sheet of paper covered with what looked like cinnamon sugar. Like Solomon's seal, cinnamon often worked to give extra strength to a spell. Not that the twins needed extra strength in their spells. They gave it to each other already, their ghost-channeling skills even stronger than Tía Paloma's because of the way they lent each other strength.

Alma and Belén were each other's best friends—another special case, which meant Leo was officially out of people to use as examples to prove Marisol and Isabel wrong. Even with the sun reaching full strength overhead, chasing away the last remnants of the cool Texas morning, Leo shivered.

She slipped back into the kitchen before Alma or Belén could see her. She didn't want to interrupt their flawless cooperation, or hear another lecture. Inside she breathed in the heavy warmth of baked and unbaked bread. She watched Mamá pop two plastic-wrapped trays into the walk-in refrigerator, wipe her hands on her apron, and then look around the kitchen and smile.

"It's good to be back where I belong," she said.

Leo's insides lumped together like oatmeal. Would Mamá agree with Isabel, that friends were a luxury a bruja couldn't afford? Would she say that Caroline didn't belong in the bakery, or in Leo's life?

"Hi there, 'jita." Mamá opened her arms to Leo. "Paloma told me you were such a big help this weekend. We still have so much to do before the sixth, and I'm counting on you to run the register. Right?"

Leo felt frozen to the ground as she leaned into Mamá's hug. She should listen to Marisol, run out the front door to chase Caroline down, and apologize. But she didn't want to let Mamá down, or Tía

Paloma, or everyone who counted on her help at the bakery. She nodded. "Right, Mamá. I can do it."

Leo knew how Caroline was hurting. She knew what it felt like to feel left out and out of place. But that understanding was exactly why she couldn't follow Marisol's advice. She never wanted to feel that way again.

She didn't want to choose at all. But she would always choose her family.

CHAPTER 5
SURPRISE

Leo slept badly that night, but she woke up worse.

At first she thought it was the beam of bright sunlight slipping through her blinds and creeping under her eyelids that made her wake with a start. The birds outside her window too seemed to chirp with extra-sharp notes that dug past her pillow and into her ear. Even the smell of her bed seemed wrong—not bad, but different, like a hotel pillow. But as she wrinkled her nose, scrunched up her eyes, and rolled over, something large and unmattresslike moved with her, and Leo's eyes snapped open.

Before her was a face, staring down at her, with

a wide pair of black-hole eyes.

"Leonora," Abuela said, her hand shaking Leo's shoulder with more weight and strength than a ghost should have. "I think you'd better get up."

Leo bolted upright. "Abuela?" She didn't have the power to see ghosts on her own, so she must be dreaming. But she didn't feel like she was dreaming. She pushed sticky curls off her forehead and licked her dry lips. In dreams, she didn't usually notice that she really needed to brush her teeth. "What are you doing here? What's going on?"

"That's what I woke you up to ask, Leonora." Abuela still sat on the bed, her dark eyes still boring into Leo, and her navy sweater still buttoned over her gray skirt. She wasn't see-through or glowing, and she didn't have bones peeking through her skin or anything to show she wasn't a living person. She looked just like she had the last time Leo had seen her, when Alma and Belén had used their powers to summon her into the room a couple months ago.

Alma and Belén's powers . . .

"Abuela!" Leo sat up straight and grabbed her dead grandmother's hand. "This must be my birth-order power! I got it, finally! I'm just like Alma and Belén. I can see you!"

She looked around the room, confusion turning into heart-pounding excitement that shot through her like a sugar rush as she searched for more ghosts. The light coming through the window made sparkling diamonds against the wall, and the bird-song made her want to jump to her feet and dance with joy. No more waiting until she was fifteen, wondering what power she would get as the first-ever fifth-born girl in the history of her family. No more feeling jealous watching Marisol and Mamá pluck items out of thin air or Isabel change the mood at the kitchen table, and no more wondering what secrets Tía Paloma and the twins were keeping.

Leo could see ghosts!

The thought was a little scary. Would Leo become like Tía Paloma now, her head always busy some-where else and her attention scattered by all the invisible spirits talking to her? How many ghosts were there? Would they always wake her up?

"Leonora." Abuela interrupted Leo's bouncing thoughts. Her arms crossed, and she stared at Leo with serious eyes. "If this is your power, it isn't like any of your sisters' abilities."

"What do you mean?"

"I mean," Abuela said, "this." She stood up, raised an arm, and slapped the wall so hard Leo jumped.

Several small orange objects fluttered out of the place where her hand met the wall, soft ovals that collected on Leo's pillow. "You're not seeing ghosts," Abuela said, "because I'm not one. Not anymore. I'm here. I'm solid. Leonora, what did you do?"

"Me?" Leo yelped. "I didn't do anything." She knelt on her bed, leaning closer to Abuela until she could see wisps of white hair coming out of her bun and curling around her ears.

Abuela scoffed and took a clumsy step backward. "Well somebody did, because one second I was having a perfectly pleasant time in el Otro Lado, and the next I'm being pulled through the veil, and here I am, in your room!"

The veil? Otro Lado? Leo didn't know what any of it meant, but as her abuela scooted backward, her feet kicked up bits of orange that swirled around the floor. Leo leaned off the side of the bed to pick up a handful . . . to find that they were soft orange flower petals. They broke in her fingers, releasing more of the scent that had woken her up.

They were marigolds—the flowers placed on altars during Día de los Muertos.

Leo stared wide-eyed at Abuela, who shrugged, causing a few petals to flutter off her shoulders and join the rest on the floor.

"I can't seem to stop shedding them. Leonora, whatever is happening, we have to find out what it is and how to reverse it. And quickly—there are some lines that shouldn't be crossed."

Leo was confused, scared, and still only half awake, which may have been why she was brave or grumpy enough to meet Abuela's stern glare with one of her own. "I didn't cross any lines." She threw off her covers, planted her feet on the floor, and stood as tall as she could to look her short Abuela straight in the eye. "And if you're going to be in the real world for now, you should just call me Leo."

Her grandmother held her gaze for a moment, then clicked her tongue with a softened expression. "Growing up to be just like Isabel, I see."

"You mean Marisol?" Leo guessed.

"Oh, hush." Abuela waved a hand, scattering more flower petals. "I'm dead, not senile. I mean your *Tía* Isabel. This is just the kind of mess she would make. She never knew when to stop pushing the boundaries of her power."

From what Leo could tell, Abuela was the one making a mess, blowing flower petals all over her room, but she kept that thought to herself. She checked the clock on her bedside table and found that it was 7:06 a.m., just a few minutes away from her alarm. She and Marisol weren't on early-morning duty today; they were supposed to join the rest of their family at the bakery later to help set up display shelves and run the register once the morning rush got started. Which left Leo with only one option.

"Come on," she said, taking Abuela's hand and tugging her toward the door. "I'm going to prove to you that this isn't my fault."

Leo peeked out of her room, nervous even though she knew Mamá and most of her sisters were gone. She walked from her room at the end of the hall to Isabel and Marisol's shared room, Abuela's shiny black shoes clacking against the wood floor. Her older sisters' door was open, showing Isabel's spotless desk and neatly made bed. When Leo peeked farther into the room where Marisol's bed was, a lump of wrinkled gray sheets and bunched black blankets squirmed.

"Marisol?" Leo whispered. "Are you up?"

"My alarm doesn't go off for three more minutes," Marisol's voice grumbled out from her nest. "This better be good, cucaracha."

"Get up, perezosa," Abuela said, crossing the room to shake a lumpy section of the bed that might have been Marisol's shoulder. "Didn't I teach you that God helps the early riser?" She turned to frown at Leo.

"That saying sounds terrible in English." She shook the blankets harder. "Wake up, my sinvergüenza."

Like a mummy rising from its sarcophagus, Marisol sat up. She untangled herself from her blankets and blinked her puffy eyes at Abuela.

Then she screamed, flailed, and fell off the bed.

"Leo, what did you *do*?"

Marisol was not the person Leo would have picked to tell about Abuela first. Her sixteen-year-old sister was out of bed now, pacing back and forth across Isabel's side of the room, where the floor was cleaner.

"I didn't do anything," Leo said, for the second time that morning, her voice turning shrill as her confidence sank. Was it possible to cast a spell completely by accident? "I mean, I don't think I did. . . . What kind of spell would do this?"

Marisol's pacing shifted as she inspected Abuela, circling her at a distance as though she was made of live snakes.

"Stop that." Abuela crossed her arms and glared at Marisol, who glared right back. "I'm your abuela, not a museum exhibit."

"You're dead," Marisol snapped. "I don't understand. Do you have a pulse? Is your . . . is your hip still broken?" She grimaced as she asked the question, took another step back, and continued her wide circular pacing.

Abuela shook her head. "I feel perfect. No ailments or injuries, even my arthritis. Fingernails normal length. No smell—I don't smell, do I?"

She glanced at Leo, who hesitated, not sure if the scent of marigolds counted.

"Well, I'm definitely not rotting," Abuela said. "So we know that much, at least."

"Know what?" Leo asked.

"That she's not, *you know*." Marisol held her hands straight out in front of her with her fingers curled into talons. "A zombie."

"I'm not raised from the grave," Abuela corrected. "Which, trust me, you should appreciate. Necromancy brings a lot of troubles, and the stink is the least of them."

"I guess . . ." Marisol approached, close enough to pat Abuela's shoulder. "But you're pretty solid for a ghost."

Señor Gato, the Logroños' big black cat, chose that moment to pad into the room, yawning. As soon as he stepped on a marigold petal he stopped, his nose twitching and the fur of his tail puffing out. He whipped his head to stare at Abuela, then gave a loud hiss and darted into the hallway as fast as Leo had ever seen him move.

"I've never seen him act like that when Alma and Belén talk to ghosts," Marisol said, her voice shaking a little.

"I'm still a spirit," Abuela said. "The cempazuchitl petals tell me that much. I've just been . . . pulled through, into the physical world. Very strange, as the cat was smart enough to notice. I've never known our magic to work this way."

Leo shrugged and looked at Marisol, who had finally come to a halt in front of Isabel's desk and now pressed her palms flat against it. "This is not good," she whispered. "This is really bad."

The knot in Leo's stomach tightened as she watched her sister's shoulders rise and fall like she had just finished five laps around the football field in PE. Isabel had told Leo once that Marisol was afraid of magic, but Leo had barely believed her. What was there to be afraid of?

"It's okay," Leo said. "It's going to be okay. Isn't it?"

Abuela put a hand on Marisol's shoulder. Marisol jumped, then froze, then took a shaky breath. "It is," she said. She turned around and, after a moment of hesitation, linked arms with her grandmother.

"Sorry, Abuela. It really is good to see you. It's just . . . you know. You're not supposed to be here!" Marisol tossed her head and snorted. "This is all going to become my fault when Mamá hears about it, just you wait."

"Why don't you girls get dressed?" Abuela asked. "I can make some breakfast."

Marisol tilted her head to one side, the furrows of her forehead flattening. "French toast?" she asked.

"I'll meet you in the kitchen," Abuela said. "As long as I have this strange body, I may as well put it to good use."

"Can you see if there's coffee in that pot?" Abuela asked Marisol as Leo entered the kitchen. Her older sister's plate held two slices of French toast already, and two more sizzled in the frying pan on the stove. Orange petals drifted across the kitchen floor whenever Abuela moved. "If I have to go back to walking everywhere, I deserve some coffee to keep me going."

"I think Daddy finished it before he left," Marisol said. A smile cracked her grim expression. "We weren't exactly expecting you, or we would have made two or three extra pots."

Leo smiled as her grandmother laughed brightly. She didn't know Abuela had loved coffee when she was alive, and it made her happy to learn it. She stopped in front of the stove to sniff the frying pan. She didn't know Abuela made such delicious French toast either.

What she knew about Abuela came mostly from stories and pictures. She had heard about the time Abuela marched into Rose Hill Elementary to fight with a teacher for confiscating Tía Paloma's markers: "If your lessons were interesting, she wouldn't be coloring in class, would she?" She had heard how Abuela lured mice and cockroaches away from the bakery gently but threw shoplifting teenagers out roughly. She had heard that Abuela used to carry gummy candies in her purse to feed to Isabel and Marisol, but that by the time the twins were born she had switched to healthier fruit snacks.

"That was really good," Marisol sighed, swiping the last bit of syrup off her plate, "but this is really bad. We need to figure out how to get you back where you came from, Abuela."

"I agree," Abuela said, flipping the slices of bread onto a plate and handing them to Leo.

In spite of the delicious smell, Leo frowned. Alma and Belén talked to ghosts all the time and nobody thought it was bad. Why did they have to rush to send Abuela back? Marisol hated magic on principle, but she was happy enough to eat Abuela's breakfast. In fact, as Marisol prepared a new pot of coffee, Leo wondered if there was any way to repeat the spell that had brought her abuela back. Could this really be her birth power? The ability to bring back departed souls? Alma and Belén could send messages between living and dead loved ones, but how much better would it be to bring them together for real? If Tía Paloma could let Tía Isabel back into her room, or if Caroline's mom . . .

"I guess we need to get to the bakery," Marisol said, perching on a stool as the coffee dripped. "I don't love the idea of driving you around town"—she gestured at Abuela—"because someone might recognize you, and that would be tough to explain. But I think we're better off going anyway. Chances are we'll need supplies from the bakery to fix this mess, and besides needing their help, I think Mamá and Tía Paloma are going to want to see this in person." She cringed, hunching her shoulders like she was already hiding from Mamá and Tía Paloma's questions. "The sooner we get to the bakery, the sooner we can send you back."

"I like that plan," Leo said quickly. Maybe meeting with the rest of the family would calm Marisol enough that she could see how it might be good to have Abuela here. Maybe Mamá or Tía Paloma could figure out if this was her power—if it was, it couldn't be bad.

Abeula nodded. "Of course, girls, you're absolutely right." But her eyes lingered on the half-full coffee pot, and she made no move to leave the kitchen.

"Well, there's no rush," Marisol said, her shoulders relaxing slightly. "We can wait ten minutes for you to drink your coffee."

Abuela's eyes crinkled as she smiled. "There are certainly benefits to existing as an intangible spirit in el Otro Lado," she said. "Like never getting hungry or thirsty. But I have missed this. The closest I can get is tasting the memory of coffee when you put it on my ofrenda." She bustled to the refrigerator for the cream, more petals floating to the ground behind her. Leo was kicking them into a pile, planning to sweep them up before before they left, but as she scanned the floor for more marigolds, something by the windowsill behind the sink caught her eye.

"Abuela?" she asked. "Did you go outside at all this morning?"

Abuela's hands cupped her coffee mug as she inhaled the scent of the drink. "No, I told you, I was pulled into your room. I woke you up as soon as it happened."

"Weird." Leo stood on her tiptoes to lean over the sink, looking past Mamá's mini herb garden to inspect the distinctive orange petal stuck to the outside of the glass. She was going to ask another question, but a knock on the front door interrupted her.

"I'll grab it." Marisol jumped in front of Abuela as she turned toward the front of the house. "You stay here and drink your coffee." She didn't exactly say "Make no noise and pretend you don't exist," but Leo was pretty sure Abuela got the message anyway.

Leo turned her attention back to the marigold petal on the windowpane. In January, even with the mild Texas weather, most flowers wouldn't be blooming outside.

"Hello?" Marisol's voice came from the front room. "If you're looking for my mom, you're better off going to the bakery during business hours."

"My goodness." It was the voice of an old lady, probably a friend of Mamá's coming to place a special order. "Isabel?"

"Nope, I'm the other one," Marisol said. Then, in a more polite voice, she added, "I'm her sister Marisol."

Leo tapped the window where the petal was, a terrible thought working its way into her head.

Holding up a hand to keep Abuela where she was, Leo ventured out of the kitchen and toward the front door.

"My goodness," the old woman repeated, looking Marisol up and down. Her dark brown skin wrinkled into deep laugh lines around her mouth, and her white hair curled in a puff above her head. Growing up in a town as small as Rose Hill, Leo was used to seeing the same faces week after week at the bakery, church, the grocery store, and school. Tourists would sometimes come to the Day of the Dead festival in November, or stretch their legs by wandering down Main Street during a summer road trip, but mostly Rose Hill was quiet and familiar. And Leo was sure she'd never seen the woman standing at the door before.

"Isabel isn't here right now, and neither is my mom," Marisol explained. Leo could hear irritation creeping into her voice. "If you're looking for them, you should head over to the bakery." She made to close the front door, but the woman didn't move. In fact, she held herself unnaturally still, not even shifting her weight.

"But you know . . . you must be fifteen, at least?" the woman asked, squinting from behind the large square rims of her glasses. *She definitely knows about brujería,* Leo thought.

Marisol huffed, her eyes narrowing like Señor Gato when Leo petted his fur the wrong way. "I'm almost seventeen."

"So you can help me," the woman said quickly. "I need your help."

Marisol blinked and didn't answer, but Leo stepped closer to the door. "Help with what?"

The old woman's eyes flicked to Leo, but her body remained stiff and still. "You're definitely not fifteen," she said with a slight frown.

"It's okay," Leo said. "I'm initiated."

"Oh." The woman looked to Marisol, who nodded. "Well, if you're sure . . . I need your help . . . with this."

All at once she lifted her arms, kicked her long flowing skirt, and shook her head. An avalanche of orange flowers blew into the house. Marisol yelped and jumped back.

It was another spirit.

Leo's heart sank.

"Leticia Morales?" At the smell of marigolds, Abuela must have decided it was safe to peek her head around the kitchen doorway. "Leti, I should have known! You always did like to make an entrance."

The spirit stepped inside, beaming wide. "Lucy! Thank goodness!" She swept past an ashen Marisol and into the house, leaving a trail of orange as she pulled Abuela into an embrace. "And don't start with me," she warned. "I mean, tell me this doesn't make you feel fabulous." She wiggled her arms again to release another shower of golden orange.

A streak of black fur swept past the two spirits, under Marisol's legs, and out the door, yowling as it went. Señor Gato curled up under his favorite bush in the front yard, his ears laid back as he eyed the two spirit invaders in his house.

Marisol looked at Leo. Her eyes were huge and her forehead wrinkled. "Leo, what did you *do*?"

CHAPTER 6

DEL OTRO LADO

Abuela and her spirit friend sat at the kitchen table, sipping coffees and shedding flower petals and chatting in fast Spanish.

" . . . del Otro Lado . . ."

" . . . Diez años . . . me morí . . ."

" . . . la magia . . ."

"¿ . . . Y Nalleli? ¿Anda echando flores por el ombligo como nosotras?"

Marisol paced from the table to the stove, her restless steps kicking up the petals left on the floor until she almost looked like a spirit herself. "Obviously we can't hide them," she muttered. "There's no way we can figure this out on our own—I mean, I'm definitely not messing with it, and you're . . ." Marisol glanced at Leo. "So that means we need to call Mamá." Her voice rose with determination. "Right now."

She paused, spinning her cell phone in her hands, but didn't dial.

Leo watched her sister do another lap around the kitchen. Marisol's anxiety made her feel calmer by comparison, but she had to admit that the appearance of Abuela's friend was alarming. Nobody else's birth-order power got away from them like this, did it? She had never heard of young Mamá or Marisol making objects pop out of thin air uncontrollably. She wondered if her family would be disappointed in her, if they would agree with Marisol that her birth-order power was a problem that needed to be solved.

She wished she could talk to Caroline.

"Give it to me; I'll call." Leo's stomach twisted with nerves, but she had learned her lesson about keeping spell problems to herself instead of asking for her family's help.

Marisol clutched her phone to her chest. "You don't understand," she snapped. "I used to study with Alma and Belén when they were first learning their powers. Tía Paloma was . . . very clear on raising the dead."

"They're spirits, not zombies," Leo reminded her sister, but the idea still made her shiver. "What . . . what did she say?"

"Nothing good," Marisol whispered while Abuela and the other spirit laughed. "We should fix this, fast. And also, it's really important that nobody outside of the family recognizes them. Okay, Leo? That would be a serious disaster."

Leo scowled at her sister, though she wasn't sure if she was mad at Marisol for suggesting that she couldn't keep a secret or at herself for thinking of calling Caroline for help.

"So let's stick with the plan," Leo said. "Get to the bakery, get everyone's heads together, and figure out a way to make them ghosts again. The invisible kind." She caught Marisol by the wrist as she passed. "Now let me call."

"Wait!" Marisol chewed her lip. "I thought of another problem."

Leo couldn't say that she was surprised. She threw up her hands, catching Abuela's attention enough to finally draw her away from her old friend.

"What is it, Marisol?" Abuela asked. "We're ready to go when you girls are."

"Well," Marisol said, "I know the bakery has the ingredients we might need to reverse this, but maybe it's irresponsible to run right into the center of town with all of this going on. I mean, if ghosts are going to pop up next to Leo, it's better for them to do it here than in the middle of Main Street, right?"

Leo's stomach dropped. Abuela pursed her lips as she considered. The other spirit looked around, her face confused. "But I didn't pop up next to Leo. I came from my son's house, on Wide Oak Lane. In the dark, he was convinced I was a burglar. Scared me out of the house with his banging and stomping around."

Marisol and Abuela stared at the old woman.

"That doesn't make sense," Marisol said.

"That does make sense." Abuela nodded slowly.

"What does that mean?" Leo asked. "If you came here from Wide Oak Lane, how did you get *there*?"

"I told you," Abuela said, rising from her stool to refill her coffee mug. "I was just pulled through, into your room, with no warning. I'm sure it was the same for you, Leti, no?"

Her spirit friend nodded.

"Pulled from where?" Leo demanded.

Abuela thought for a moment, then said, "I

always called it el Otro Lado. The other side, the spirit world. It exists alongside this one, but separated. The boundary can be malleable, stretching or thinning on Día de los Muertos, and on death anniversaries and birthdays. It can be seen through by brujas like your aunt or your twin sisters, and can even allow communication on special occasions and with the right spells. But it shouldn't break. It shouldn't let things, especially spirits, slip through. That's a type of magic our family has never meddled in. The boundary exists for a reason."

"Well, Leo's never met a boundary she didn't ignore," Marisol said.

Leo shook her head. "I didn't break any boundaries," she said. "I didn't *do* anything." She felt like her brain was trapped in a microwave, spinning around and around. How could this be her birth power if she didn't know she was doing it? How could she bring spirits to life all the way across town? What if the words she kept repeating were really true—what if this wasn't her fault?

If Leo hadn't caused this, something must have. Even if no one else believed her, Leo was determined to get to the bottom of the mystery.

"Abuela," she said, "and . . ."

"Mrs. Morales," Abuela said, at the same time

the other spirit introduced herself as "Leticia, but call me Leti."

The introduction clicked a connection in Leo's brain. "Morales? Do you know Tricia Morales?"

Abuela smiled, and Mrs. Morales laughed loud as she nodded. "My granddaughter," she said. "Such a good girl. Of course you two would be friends!"

Leo smiled. Tricia was in her reading group at school, and one of the founding members of the lunchtime snacks and baking club. The girls had known each other since kindergarten, but Leo had never known their grandmothers were friends.

"It was so hard to leave her," Mrs. Morales said softly, not really speaking to Leo anymore. "She was only a toddler, but she was there in the hospital at the end of my life, crying because she couldn't climb into the bed with me. There were so many people there, doctors and nurses and things, and I wanted to tell her that I loved her, that I would stay with her if I could, but . . ."

Mrs. Morales sighed. Leo's chest ached as she pictured baby Tricia in the hospital.

"I'm sure she doesn't remember," Mrs. Morales continued. "She's so smart and so good on the clarinet. And she's handling things with her parents so well. . . ." Abuela patted Mrs. Morales's arm.

Leo knew Mrs. Morales was probably right that Tricia didn't remember her grandmother's passing. Like Leo, Tricia probably had no memories of her grandmother at all. Was it better or worse to not even know the sadness of losing your loved one? Leo shook her head to clear it. She needed to be an investigator. She didn't need to be sad for her friend and the grandmother she barely remembered.

But . . . the boundary kept Leo from knowing Abuela, and Tricia from knowing Leticia Morales. It took Tía Isabel away from Tía Paloma, and Mrs. Campbell away from Caroline. When Leo thought about it, this boundary didn't seem like such a great thing.

"Was there anything you were both doing in el Otro Lado?" Marisol asked, twisting her fingers through her hair. "Something you have in common?"

The two women exchanged glances. "It's difficult to explain," Mrs. Morales said slowly. "El Otro Lado is . . . different."

"Please, can you try?" Leo looked at Abuela.

Abuela set down her coffee mug. "In el Otro Lado," she said with a sigh, "the easiest thing to be is, well, everything. Being one specific thing, being just yourself, takes so much effort. It's exhausting. But I was being myself when I was pulled through."

Leo wasn't sure how spirits could exist without being themselves, and Marisol's tilted head suggested that her sister was just as confused.

"Me too!" Mrs. Morales said. "I had just drawn myself out of the everything and had taken this form." She smiled the same hopeful smile that Leo's teacher, Ms. Wood, always gave after explaining a problem.

"What does that mean?" Leo asked. "'Being everything'?" She had never thought much about what happened to someone after they died. She had worried about losing her family, especially when Caroline's mom got sick, but it was always from the viewpoint of the living people being left behind. For as long as she could remember, Mamá would mention spirits the way everyone talked about them on Día de los Muertos, like they were just normal relatives coming for a visit from far away. Learning about her family's magic, seeing Alma and Belén chat with Abuela and other ancient family members, had confirmed Leo's belief that death wasn't that much different from life. She remembered being in church once, hearing the padre mention heaven, and asking Mamá about it after mass. She had imagined that heaven was like a mirror image of Earth built out of clouds. She never imagined that you could stop being yourself when you died.

"I'm sorry," Mrs. Morales said. "It really is impossible to describe to people who are alive."

"Everything is so rigid on this side of the veil." Abuela nodded in agreement. "And you have to use human languages to communicate everything, which is so limiting."

"Oh, I know!" Mrs. Morales slapped the table, raising a puff of petals. "I had so much trouble trying to express myself that I left a note for my son, Freddy. Now, how did I describe it . . . ?"

"You did what?" Marisol's mouth hung open. "You wrote him a note?" Her voice jumped higher with each sentence.

"Yes," Mrs. Morales said. "And I'm sure I explained it better than we're doing now."

Leo looked at her older sister, her low-level worry finally coming to a bubbling boil. "You wrote him a note about coming back from the dead?"

"From el Otro Lado," Mrs. Morales corrected.

Marisol whimpered.

"Did he read it?" Leo asked. Maybe there would be a heartwarming story, just the thing to prove that the spirits being here wasn't such a huge disaster. Or maybe he had called the police and they were coming to get Leo right now and arrest her for summoning spirits.

"Well, I'm sure he hasn't seen it yet. I snuck back into the house and left it on the counter after he went to work."

Abuela gave her friend a steely frown. "Leti, how could you be so reckless?"

Mrs. Morales huffed in response. "What should I have done? I didn't want him to spend all day worrying about home invaders! And there's something . . . very important I need him to know. You don't know what it's like, Lucy. You get to speak to your girls whenever you want. This might be my only opportunity."

Mrs. Morales had a point. After dealing with her family's lying and hiding their magic for years, Leo understood being fed up with secrets. But still, Mamá and Tía Paloma had both asked Leo not to spread word of the family's powers, and Isabel had explained why it was important. How angry would they all be if it turned out that Leo had summoned a bunch of blabbermouth spirits and let the magic out of the bag?

Well, maybe summoning the spirits wasn't Leo's fault. But if she didn't do something to stop Mrs. Morales now, it would be her fault if Tricia's dad traced all this magic back to the Logroños. Had the family ever uninitiated someone?

"Okay." Marisol's face was grim. "New priority. We're getting that note."

"I can do it," Leo said. "I've been to Tricia's house. It's only a few minutes from here, if you can drive me."

Abuela picked up her coffee and drained the mug with a determined nod. She hushed Mrs. Morales when she started to grumble. "Leti, te quiero mucho, but you have to know that this isn't right. A note is just going to confuse and scare Freddy, maybe his whole family. These things have to be done delicately."

Mrs. Morales still looked like she wanted to argue.

"Once we get rid of the note," Marisol told her, "we can ask Tía Paloma how to get a message to your son in a less startling way. She's an expert at ghost communication. She'll know what to do."

Mrs. Morales hesitated, then shrugged. She let herself be towed by Marisol, who grabbed each spirit by the elbow and rushed them toward the back door.

"We can discuss this in the car," she said. "Oh, and here." She let go of Abuela to toss Leo her cell phone. "While we're driving, text Isabel that we'll be on our way to the bakery soon with a . . . magical problem. And maybe tell her that if she can start *softening up* Mamá and Tía Paloma, that would be great."

Leo's mouth dropped open. Marisol was asking Isabel to use her powers?

"Oh, don't look at me like that," Marisol grumbled. "We have enough to worry about right now. Might as well use whatever advantage we've got."

CHAPTER 7
THE HEIST

The Morales's house wasn't far from Leo's—walking distance, if they hadn't been trying to keep two spirits out of sight. Leo had been visiting Tricia ever since they had all started a lunchtime snack club in November. Usually the walk was a comforting tour of the short brick houses that made up Leo's neighborhood. She would wave at Mrs. Jones, who always sat in her rocking chair, her white hair and skin making her look like a larger version of the stone statues filling her front yard. She would cut across the empty lot on Elm Drive, hopping over the tall grass and trying to spot the stray cat that lived in the bushes. But today they needed to get there fast.

Again, Leo found herself wishing that Caroline was here to help with the plan. The two of them could definitely cook up a way to get Mrs. Morales's note without raising any suspicions.

Leti Morales giggled as she and Abuela climbed into the back of Mamá's van. "Lucy, do you remember when we used to get rides with Miguel Antonio and his sister? The one with the hair?"

Abuela laughed loud and sharp, but she fell silent when Marisol shot the two old women a reproachful look from the driver's seat.

"This isn't a field trip," Marisol barked.

Abuela nodded. But after a few moments had passed, she leaned to her friend and whispered, loud enough for Leo to hear, "I was thinking more of you driving in Alfredo's convertible."

Marisol didn't respond to the hushed giggles except by pulling out of the driveway with a squeal of tires. Leo gripped her seatbelt tightly with one hand and typed a message to Isabel with the other, her pulse racing faster than the car as she imagined her oldest sister reading the message. Like Abuela had told Mrs. Morales, some news just didn't seem appropriate to deliver in writing.

She finally sent a message using Marisol's wording to let Isabel know that "a magical problem" was afoot, without specifically mentioning the spirits.

Mrs. Morales rolled down the back window, her eyes closed and smile wide as the wind rippled her curly hair and sent marigold petals flying out to float on the puddles left from yesterday's rain.

"Stop that," Marisol snapped, rolling the window back up and punching the child-safety lock button sharply. Silent laughter from the back seat shook the van.

Leo tapped her own window, wishing the spirits would help her plan instead of being silly. Would Tricia be home? It was still early, so she might be asleep, but could Leo make it into the house without waking her friend? And how would she explain herself if she got caught?

They pulled onto Tricia's block before she could come up with satisfactory answers. Marisol stopped the van on the curb and Abuela and Mrs. Morales fell silent. Leo gulped.

The Moraleses lived in a one-story beige brick house with azalea bushes along the front wall and the blue triangle of a Puerto Rican flag hanging in the window. Mr. Morales's repair shop and used-car lot, which was a few blocks away on the road toward Main Street, also had US, Texan, and Mexican flags in addition to Puerto Rican ones, the four symbols circling the fence and beckoning customers in with their friendly waves.

"What now?" Marisol asked. "Do you think anyone's home?"

"There's no car in the garage," Leo pointed out.

"I saw Freddy and Olivia leave for work," Mrs. Morales added.

"What about Tricia?" Marisol asked.

Mrs. Morales bit her lip and shook her head.

Marisol raked a hand through her hair. "Well, where did you leave the note?"

After a quick bout of bickering and glaring, Marisol convinced Leo that it would be less weird if she just knocked on the front door. "If she doesn't answer, then we can assume she's asleep or out of the house, and we can start considering how best to try sneaking in. But if she answers, you can still make this work. Pretend you have a question about school or something."

Leo nodded. It didn't sound so hard when Marisol said it. Get into the living room where Mrs. Morales had left the note, grab it before Tricia could get a good look at it. Simple.

"She might see me grab it," she thought out loud. "So I should have something to replace it with."

Marisol nodded. She flexed her right hand a few times and then pinched her fingers together and plucked them backward. A sheet of notebook paper emerged from thin air, and Marisol repeated the motion to produce a pen, which she used to scribble a list of groceries.

Leo tried not to envy her sister's easy use of her birth power. She took a deep breath, stashed Marisol's list up the sleeve of her green hoodie, and hopped out of the car. Her stomach twisted in knots and her brain swirled with everything that could go wrong, but she marched up to the front door anyway and knocked.

Nothing. She knocked again, waited another minute, and then knocked a third time, softly. Maybe Tricia wasn't home. She glanced over her shoulder at the van. If no one answered, she would return and ask Marisol to use her power to make a lock pick or something to help her get inside the house. Except Leo didn't know how to use a lock pick, so maybe that wasn't a great idea. Before she could make up her mind, though, the door rattled and creaked open just an inch.

Tricia squinted through the crack, brown eyes fluttering to stay open.

"Leo? What are you doing here?" She opened the door all the way, revealing fuzzy pink pajama pants and a dark brown ponytail that puffed in several different directions. "What time is it?"

"Hi," Leo said. She smiled wide, but her face began to heat up as she realized she had no idea what to say next. "Um . . . Hi. It's, like, eight thirty, I think."

"Okay." Tricia rubbed a hand over her face. Now that she knew Mrs. Morales, Leo could see how Tricia resembled her grandmother, with the same round cheeks and arched eyebrows. "So . . . what's up?"

"Nothing much," Leo responded automatically. Tricia tilted her head. "Oh, I mean, actually, I came here to ask you about . . ." School didn't even start up again for another four days. What was Leo supposed to pretend to need? "I just wanted to . . ." She searched her brain for a lie, any lie, and came up empty.

Tricia frowned. "Are you okay? What's wrong?"

"I'm fine. Everything's fine," Leo answered too quickly.

"So you knocked on my door first thing in the morning in the middle of winter break to tell me the time and say that everything's fine?" Tricia asked skeptically.

"I . . ." Leo opened and closed her mouth. She couldn't do this. She needed Caroline to be here, coming up with creative lies.

She needed Caroline.

That was it.

"I got in a big fight with Caroline yesterday," Leo blurted. "My family thinks she hangs around the bakery too much, and so I was a jerk to her when she came by and I hurt her feelings really bad, and I'm scared she hates me now."

"Oh no," Tricia said. "I'm sorry! Do you want to come in? I've got Froot Loops."

Leo followed Tricia inside. While her friend closed the door, Leo caught a glimpse of the van, which Marisol had backed up so it was parked several houses down. Marisol raised a hand in a thumbs-up. Leo's stomach flipped over guiltily. She was getting to be a pretty good liar on her own.

"So what happened?" Tricia asked, walking to the kitchen and offering a bowl and a box of cereal.

Leo wished Tricia's house was laid out more like Caroline's, with the living room connecting all the other parts of the house. But maybe it was lucky that Tricia's house had the kitchen at the center of everything instead, since it meant Tricia might not have seen the note yet.

Now Leo just had to get to it.

She poured herself some Froot Loops but left the

milk on the counter, popping a few of the dry rings into her mouth. "Thanks," she said. Buying time as she worked out how to tell the story of her fight without mentioning magic.

"No worries. I'm sorry everything's a mess." Tricia swiped a pile of white paper bags and plastic bottles off the kitchen table and into a drawer next to the sink. "This week's been really . . ." She shrugged and poured milk over her cereal.

Leo crunched more Froot Loops, her mind flashing through possibilities. The bathroom was on the other side of the house, opposite the living room. Could she pretend to be using it, sneak past Tricia, and get to the note without getting caught? It seemed risky.

"Leo?" Tricia waved a hand. "Earth to Leo?"

Leo swallowed her mouthful of dry cereal and coughed. "Sorry, what?"

"Do you want to talk about Caroline?" Tricia asked. "It's okay if you don't, but you seemed like you wanted to."

Leo nodded. "Right. Um, can I just use your bathroom first?"

"Of course." Tricia picked up her bowl and walked Leo to the hallway.

"I know, I know. Second door on the left," Leo

tried to assure her friend, but Tricia followed her anyway. Leo closed the bathroom door and waited, but instead of footsteps she heard the crunch of Froot Loops. No chance of sneaking into the living room while Tricia waited in the hall.

Okay. Leo met her eyes in the long bathroom mirror. *You can do this.* Tricia hadn't seen the note yet. Everything was absolutely going to work out.

Her face in the mirror didn't look so certain.

Being in the bathroom made Leo need to go to the bathroom. She turned away from the mirror—and jumped about three feet in the air. Orange petals littered the sill of the frosted-glass window above the toilet, and fingers slipped under the crack to wiggle open the window latch.

"Mrs. Morales?" Leo climbed carefully onto the toilet seat to open the window. "What the heck are you doing?" she whispered. "Get back to the van!"

"What's taking so long?" Mrs. Morales asked. "Did she see the note? Can I talk to her now?"

"No!" Leo scowled. "Go away! I'm working on it."

"I have to talk to her," Mrs. Morales said. "It's very important. I have to tell her—"

"Hey!" Marisol stomped through the side yard, heading straight toward Mrs. Morales. "Get back here right now!"

Leo slammed the window shut, leaving Mrs. Morales to deal with Marisol's rage. She fake-flushed the toilet, real-washed her hands, and found Tricia eating cereal in the hallway.

"Thanks," she said as Tricia walked with her back to the kitchen. A frustrated scream built up behind her smile.

"So you know my mom's been letting me work more in the bakery?" she asked when they sat back at the kitchen table. She shoved a handful of Froot Loops into her mouth, grinding them between her teeth.

Tricia nodded. "You mentioned it when you bought the marranitos for snack club. You said you baked them yourself."

Leo smiled. "Yeah, exactly. So I've been working there after school, and Caroline comes to hang out sometimes, but my mom and my sisters have been really annoyed by it. They think she's, I don't know, a distraction. And they don't want her to help me study, um, baking techniques."

"Why? Are they, like, afraid she's going to steal secret recipes and open her own bakery?" Tricia asked.

Leo laughed weakly. "Yeah, I don't know. They're being so annoying about it, like I have to choose between my family and—" A flash of orange derailed Leo's train of thought. "And, um . . ." She watched the kitchen window carefully, and sure enough, Mrs. Morales's head soon popped over the ledge. Leo fake-coughed to cover up a shooing gesture.

"That sounds so unfair," Tricia said. "Your family should never make you feel like you're not allowed to have friends."

"Well, they're not saying . . . it's a little bit complicated." Leo struggled to defend her family without explaining the secrecy of magic.

Mrs. Morales waved her hands and pointed through the window. Leo flapped her hand back, shaking her head.

"What's wrong?" Tricia turned just as Mrs. Morales ducked out of sight.

"No, nothing. There was a mosquito." Leo fumed. "Um, you're right. My family is *the worst*." She raised her voice, hoping it could be heard through the window. "I can't believe they would do this!"

She didn't know how Mrs. Morales had escaped Marisol. She didn't know why the spirit was so determined to talk to Tricia. But Leo wasn't going to let anyone jeopardize her family's secret.

"My parents are the worst too," Tricia said, stirring green and blue milk at the bottom of the cereal bowl and watching the colors swirl. “I don’t know if I told you, but . . .”

“Do you want to watch TV?” Leo asked. She needed to get into the living room, now, and get out of here before Mrs. Morales ruined everything.

“What?” Tricia looked more confused than ever. “Uh, sure, I guess.” She picked up Leo’s empty bowl and turned toward the sink, which was right in front of Mrs. Morales’s window.

“I’ve got it!” Leo snatched both bowls out of Tricia’s hands and dropped them in the sink. From where she stood, Mrs. Morales was clearly visible, ducked just under the windowsill. The old woman waved sheepishly when Leo saw her.

Leo ran water over the bowls and took advantage of Tricia’s turned back to give Mrs. Morales her worst glare. *Go away!*

Mrs. Morales just pointed, again, at something to the left of the sink.

“You can leave them there,” Tricia said. Leo spun around and stepped away from the sink so her friend wouldn’t come any closer. “We can go to my room and watch something.”

Leo had totally forgotten that Tricia had a TV in her bedroom.

“No, um, that’s okay,” she backtracked. “We don’t

have to . . . Never mind." She plopped back into her seat at the table.

Tricia watched her with narrowed eyes, moving slowly back to her chair like someone approaching a wild animal. "That's fine," she said. "So . . . what happened yesterday?"

"What?" Leo watched the window carefully. "Yes-terday?" After a short pause, Mrs. Morales's hand rose above the windowsill and pointed again.

"Yesterday. You said Caroline came by the bak-ery?" Tricia prompted. "What are you . . . ?" She turned to look over her shoulder, following Leo's gaze.

"Nothing," Leo said. "Yes. I said that. Um, I didn't stand up for Caroline when my family was telling her, basically, that she should go home. And then she stormed out, and I haven't, um, I haven't talked to her since. . . . Did you put something in that drawer?"

Leo had finally realized that Mrs. Morales was pointing to the half-open drawer by the sink, the one Tricia had moved things into when Leo arrived.

White paper bags with long labels. Orange plas-tic bottles. Leo had seen piles like that before.

"Oh, yeah, it's just some of my parents' stuff." Tri-cia jumped up and slammed the drawer shut. "Are you sure you don't want to watch TV?"

Leo had spent a lot of time lying and hiding things lately, so it wasn't hard to recognize Tricia's quick, breathy voice. "What's going on?" she asked. The drawer was full of prescription medicine, just like when Caroline's mother had first been diagnosed. "Is someone . . . sick?"

Tricia's face collapsed like a ruined soufflé. "It's nothing," she said in a tiny voice. "You don't have to . . . You're already upset."

"No." Leo shook her head. She wasn't upset, not like Tricia. She was a faker, a sneaky jerk who was scheming while it became clear her friend had real problems. "I'm fine. I'm listening."

Listening. That was what she hadn't done since she first knocked on the door. Not since Caroline had gotten back from Costa Rica. Guilt made her squirm in her seat.

"It's my dad," Tricia said. "Something with his blood pressure, and his heart. . . . He and Mom won't tell me exactly what's happening, they just say everything is fine, but I'm not dumb, I can tell it's serious. He found out recently, except he keeps pretending like it didn't happen. And my mom says he needs to take his medication or else . . . But he doesn't listen. And I'm scared."

While Tricia talked, Mrs. Morales stood up, her hand pressed to the window as she listened. Her mouth was squeezed shut, her shoulders pulled tight together, her eyes hurting. She and Tricia looked more alike than ever, now.

"I'm sorry," Leo said. She didn't know which one she was speaking to. "I'm really sorry."

Tricia shrugged. "It's not your fault. My dad just . . . he's acting so weird about all of this. I don't know what his problem is. It's like he doesn't care about being healthy. I just wish someone could tell him to listen to his doctors and stay on his medicine and take this seriously!"

Leo hadn't asked Mrs. Morales what her note said. She had never wondered what was so important for her to tell her son. But now she suspected she knew exactly what advice the note contained.

Was she doing the wrong thing? Should she turn Tricia around, let Mrs. Morales come inside? Leo didn't want to lie and keep secrets anymore. She was tired of being a good bruja and a bad friend.

"Tricia." She tried to think of the right words. "Maybe . . . maybe there is someone who could tell your dad what to do so that he would listen."

"I know, I know." Tricia buried her face in her hands. "I just . . . I can't, Leo. I know I should, but . . . he's my dad. He always says he should be the one taking care of me, not the other way around. And every time I try, I get so nervous and awkward and—"

"Wait." Leo stopped worrying about her own guilt and focused on Tricia's words. "You haven't talked to your dad about any of this?"

In the window behind Tricia, Mrs. Morales nodded her head, rolled her eyes in a huge circular motion, and pointed wildly.

"He hasn't even talked to me about his medication," Tricia said. "I obviously know about it, because it's right here on the table. He and my mom argue about it all the time, and they're not very good at hiding their fights. But . . . he never officially told me."

"But that's . . ." Leo frowned. Mrs. Morales circled her hands to encourage her to keep talking. "You should tell him all of this. He can't just act like everything is fine."

Mrs. Morales raised her hands in the air, triumphant petals circling her head.

"Leo . . . you're right," Tricia said. "I'll make him listen. He should know how I feel, that I know what's going on. I'm going to tell him to *cut it out* already." Tricia slammed her fist on the table. Mrs. Morales danced happily behind her.

Leo beamed. "That sounds like a good idea."

"You should talk to your family too," Tricia told Leo. "About Caroline, I mean. They're being unreasonable. You should tell them so. And apologize to Caroline. I'm sure she'll be happy to hear from you."

"Yeah . . ." Leo shrugged, feeling like the world's biggest phony. Tricia was ready to be brave and tell her father the truth. Leo was still protecting her family by lying to her friends. Caroline wouldn't want to hear from her, not when Leo hadn't changed anything about her actions.

"Hang on." Tricia sniffed. "I need to get a tissue. Be right back." She stood up and turned toward the hallway. Mrs. Morales dived out of sight. "Thanks," Tricia said before she left the room.

For three seconds, alone in the kitchen, Leo hesitated. She could leave the note. She could stop lying.

But would the note make Tricia feel any better? Or would it just make her confused, or angry, or scared? And if Tricia was going to speak up and talk to her father, he wouldn't need the note anyway.

She slipped into the living room, lifted the note off the coffee table, and folded it carefully into her pocket before returning to the kitchen.

"I think I'm going to go," she said when Tricia returned with a handful of tissues. "You were right. I need to talk to my family. Thanks for listening."

"No, thank *you*," Tricia said. "I'm sorry I made everything about my own problems."

Leo almost burst out laughing. Tricia was far less guilty of that selfishness than Leo was.

"Are you sure you don't want to hang out?" Tricia asked. She wiped her still-red nose. "Mai is going to come over in a couple of hours."

"No thanks." Leo smiled. "My sister is supposed to bring me to the bakery soon. I should get back home. Tell Mai hi from me, though."

She left, waved until Tricia closed the door, then sprinted down the block to Marisol's car.

Mrs. Morales sat calmly in the back seat of the van, hands connected to the armrests with plastic zip ties and a huge smile spread across her face.

"I don't want to talk about it," Marisol said before Leo could ask about the spirit's escape.

Leo raised her eyebrows, noticing the red imprint of zip ties on Marisol's wrists.

Marisol shook her head. "I found a new useful object to summon, and it backfired at first. I really don't want to talk about it. Did you get it?"

"I got it." Leo produced the note from her pocket and handed it to Abuela, who passed it into Mrs. Morales's bound hands. "Let's go."

CHAPTER 8
DETOUR

Mrs. Morales's happiness didn't wear off as they drove toward the bakery, especially when Marisol reached back to turn the summoned zip ties back into nothing. "My granddaughter is an amazing girl," she told Abuela as the car bumped out of the neighborhood. "I felt so useless and worried before. I couldn't do anything to help Freddy, and I could see how scared he was. But now I know Tricia will work it out. She's such a good girl. And Freddy will do the right thing for her."

Abuela nodded. "You raised him right," she said.

"He's stubborn like me." Mrs. Morales sighed. "I

was never any good at being sick."

"I remember," Abuela teased. "You made me walk you home on that sprained ankle just because you thought Alfredo was babying you."

Mrs. Morales laughed. "I forgot all about that!"

"That's because you weren't the one you were leaning on," Abuela said. "I probably still have the bruises, mira."

Leo smiled in spite of her nervous stomachache. Even knowing that the spirits didn't belong here, she still liked getting to know Abuela better, listening to her joke with her friend. She was happy that Tricia had a possible solution to her problem, and that Mrs. Morales felt better. But now that the note was taken care of, Leo was back to worrying. As they drove toward the bakery, she wondered again if Mamá would blame her for the spirits' appearance. She wondered if she was really a bad friend—if Caroline would forgive her, or if Tricia would think of her differently if she knew that what Leo had told her was mostly lies.

She looked in the rearview mirror to watch the two old ladies—and gasped at what she saw.

"What?" Marisol slammed on the brakes. "What is it?"

"Abuela, your hair." Leo stared. Her grandmother's silver bun was streaked with black, and

Mrs. Morales's white hair had darkened to a salt-and-pepper gray. The two ghosts looked at each other.

"I thought I felt younger spending time with you," Abuela said, her eyes wide.

Mrs. Morales chuckled and rubbed the thinner wrinkles on her face. "Do you think we can keep this up? We'll be young enough to go dancing by the end of the night."

Marisol started driving again, her mouth a tight line. "Did you forget we're trying to keep you out of sight?" she asked.

"Of course, of course," Abuela said. "We're only joking. . . . Although, well, nobody around here would recognize us. They never knew us as young women."

"Their loss," Mrs. Morales added, and Abuela let out another burst of laughter.

Marisol pressed the gas pedal extra hard, and the van lumbered down the street with a roar.

"Can y'all duck or something?" Marisol asked as they turned onto Main Street. She nervously watched the car on their right until it pulled in front of them, then switched to eyeing Ms. Flores, who was outside sprucing up the window decorations of her restaurant. "I feel like everyone can see you."

Abuela and Mrs. Morales just giggled harder.

Tiny raindrops collected on the windshield as the car approached the bakery. When the giggling cut off suddenly, Leo perked up her ears. Mrs. Morales whispered, "¿Esos son . . . ?"

Leo glanced in the rearview mirror to see Abuela and Mrs. Morales pointing and staring at something on the other side of the car. She spun around in her seat to follow the pointing fingers.

On the sidewalk, scattered somewhat by the drizzle but leaving an unmistakable trail up to the green-awninged door of the hardware store, was a line of orange petals.

"Stop the car!" Leo shouted. Marisol shouted a curse word back, and everyone slumped forward as the brakes squealed.

"What happened?" Marisol asked. "Someone sees us, right? Someone's going to ask questions." She took several quick breaths. "Okay, we should get our stories straight. You're our aunts. Our great-aunts visiting from Mexico, and, um, Abuela had a twin sister and Mrs. Morales is related by marriage and—"

"Marisol." Leo pointed at the hardware store. "Nobody saw us, but I think there's a spirit in there. I'm going inside. Watch them." She was running as soon as her feet hit the asphalt.

The hardware store didn't have a bell, but it had an orange cat that meowed when Leo opened the door, almost catching its tail. Cannon's Hardware was a large rectangular building with aluminum walls and concrete floors, separated into sections for tools, lumber, plumbing, and other things Leo didn't know anything about. The only part of the store she'd ever visited with Mamá was the plexiglass-enclosed annex in the back, where they sold plants and gardening supplies. The line of petals, the same color as the cat who was sniffing them, led straight back to the annex.

There was a teenager in a green polo shirt sweeping marigold petals into a dustpan in front of the gardening section. His light brown skin, wavy black hair, and large ears looked familiar; Leo was sure he went to Rose Hill High School, and she thought he might even be a friend of Marisol's. Maybe it would have been better if *she* had followed the petals.

"Hi, can I help you find anything," he droned, tugging only one earbud out of his ear. He looked Leo up and down—mostly down, since he was over six feet tall. "Did you, uh, lose your parents?"

Leo opened her mouth to tell him that she was not a little kid, but then she swallowed the words as an idea ballooned out of her annoyance.

"Yes," she said. "I was with my . . . aunt? Uncle? My aunt and my uncle. I lost them, and I think one of them came in here. I'm not sure which."

The teen gave a slow shrug. "Yeah, I saw a couple people. They were in here just a minute ago, buying flowers with their kids. I didn't see what a mess they made until after they left." He nodded at the dustpan.

Leo's eyes bulged. "I don't think that was them," she squeaked, hoping that there wasn't a whole family of spirits walking the town.

"Well, then it's just been that guy." The teen pointed, then frowned. "Aw jeez, does nobody understand how to look at a flower without ripping it to shreds?"

The customer in the gardening annex stood inspecting a pair of shears, surrounded by another puddle of petals.

"That must be him!" Leo yelped. "Um, I mean, yep, that is him. Definitely."

The teen raised two bushy black eyebrows. "That's your uncle?"

The man, Leo realized a second late, was easily as old as Abuela, hunched and balding and white, with pale pink skin and rosy cheeks.

"Great-uncle," she said. "By marriage."

The kid shrugged, turning back to his dustpan.

Leo squeezed her hands together to keep them steady, hardly believing she had gotten away with her terrible lie. But she still needed to distract the store employee before she could confront the spirit. The old man might do any number of noticeable things, from spraying petals all over the place to making a big deal out of the fact that he had no idea who Leo was.

Her mind raced along with her heart. She needed a shiny distracting lie, one that would tempt the employee away from his dustpan. What did teenage boys like? She didn't spend much time with teenage boys, except her cousin J.P., who was on her dad's side of the family and liked movies about space. The only other teenage boys Leo had spent any time with were the ones who followed Marisol home and looked at her like lost puppies.

Well . . . it was worth a shot.

"Um, do you know my sister?" Leo asked the employee. "Marisol Logroño?"

His eyebrows jumped again, and his voice came out in a squeak when he said, "Oh, that's your sister?" He coughed and continued, in a lower voice, "Yeah, we have some classes together. She's cool. Whatever." The tips of his ears started to turn red. "Why?"

"Well, she's outside," Leo said. "Waiting with

my . . . other great-aunts. We're having a family reunion. For Día de los Reyes?" Leo clamped her mouth shut before she could add any more confusing details to her lie, but luckily the boy was nodding without seeming to listen, his eyes turned toward the windows at the front of the shop. She took a breath. "Anyway, she said she wanted to say hello."

"Yeah, cool. That's cool." He cleared his throat. "I should take the trash out anyway, before I have to bag all these flower petals." He left the broom propped against the wall and jogged toward the front door, only stopping to pick up the mostly empty trash can on his way out.

Leo grinned. Teenagers were too easy. Now for the old man.

"Excuse me," she said. The man didn't look up from the shears. His eyes scanned the label, mouth moving as he read. "Um, excuse me?" she repeated. "Sir?" She took another step into the annex to tap the man on the shoulder.

He startled, dropping the pair of shears. "Sakes alive," he said loudly. "Don't sneak up like that, young lady. How can I help you?"

Leo tried out her best friendly smile. "My name is Leo Logroño, and I know you came from el Otro Lado—"

"Speak up a little?" the man asked, turning to face Leo head on and leaning forward.

"Um, hi, I'm Leo. I know that you're . . ." Leo didn't want to shout about spirits. "Well, I need you to . . ." The old man stared intently at her and moved his lips along with her as she spoke, which was distracting. "Um, can you just come with me, please?"

The man nodded along with her words, but then he straightened and shook his head.

"Sorry, young lady. I'm on a mission. You wouldn't believe the state my garden is in right now! A complete mess—totally neglected! I've only been gone for half a decade or so, and it seems that nobody so much as weeded it in all that time. I know January isn't the ideal month to get one's garden back in order, but with a little luck . . ." He started back down the aisle, picking up a new pair of shears and muttering to himself about planting seasons and perennials, trailing orange petals behind him.

"No," Leo said, and then louder, "No, wait! You have to come with me." Leo gritted her teeth. "We don't have time for this."

"Just right, young lady. Which species can survive transplanting at this time of year? I don't know how long I have to get everything looking nice before I'm pulled back, after all."

"That's not what I . . ." Leo stomped her foot in frustration and almost slipped on the marigolds. If only she had Isabel's power to make him feel like doing what she needed him to do, or Marisol's power to produce spiders and wasps out of thin air—that would drive him out of the shop. Or if Caroline were here, she would know just what to say to convince him to come outside.

"Sir," she said, forcing her voice to be calm, "I know what you're talking about. I know where you were pulled from. And it's very important that you come with me right now. It's . . . sort of an emergency."

The man, squinting at a row of potted shrubs farther down the aisle, didn't even acknowledge that she had spoken. She didn't have her sisters' powers, or her friend's help, and there was no time to waste, and that meant she was going to have to get creative.

Leo caught up with the old man and tugged his sleeve until he faced her again. "Sir, what I was trying to tell you is that you should come with me . . . to the plant nursery. It's new in town, and has a much greater selection. If you really want to repair your garden, I can show you where it is." She made sure to speak up. "If you come right now, during our, um, opening weekend, you can get a twenty percent discount." Leo flashed her best salesperson smile, perfected at the bakery register. "Don't you at least want to come see our inventory?"

The old man chewed on his bottom lip. "I don't know if I like your business practices. Hiring children, stealing customers out from other stores." He looked down at the shrub in his hand, bringing it closer to his face to read the price tag. "Twenty percent, you said?"

"Opening weekend only." Leo smiled and raised her eyebrows. Her fingernails dug into her palms.

"Well, all right. I suppose I can take a look, at least. Lead the way, young lady."

Leo didn't wait for him to change his mind. She tugged him out of the annex, through the front doorway, past the boy in the green polo, who leaned against Marisol's window. Leo pulled open the door of the van and shoved the old man into the back seat. "Complimentary shuttle," she explained when he looked like he might object, and she jumped into the front seat herself. "Go, go!" she whispered to Marisol, who nodded, waved the smiling boy back from the car, and pulled away from the curb.

"This doesn't look like a shuttle," the new spirit said as Marisol revved the engine. "Where did you say the nursery was located?" When Leo couldn't think of an answer, he tapped the back of Marisol's head. "Excuse me, miss, do you work for the plant nursery?"

"Leo, what is he talking about?" Marisol asked. "Did you lie to this old man?"

Leo shrank in her seat. "He wasn't listening."

"Don't worry," Abuela told the man. "The girls are here to help. They're going to send us back across the veil."

"Send us back?" the man huffed. "But what about my garden?"

"Oh dear, this poor soul wants to tend to his garden." Mrs. Morales sighed wistfully. "Surely you'll let him do that before you send us all back, won't you? It's such a reasonable request; what could be the harm?"

"Nobody's doing anything with any gardens," Marisol said. "You're all going back the second we can work out the spell!"

"Abduction, and gross dishonesty," the old man complained at top volume. "I thought you were a nice young lady, but it turns out you're nothing but a con artist!"

Leo balled her hands into fists and counted down the blocks to the bakery to avoid the sour pit of guilt in her stomach. She didn't want to lie or keep an old man away from his garden, but the spirits had to stay hidden, and wandering around the hardware store was far from hidden.

"Watch how you talk to my granddaughter," Abuela warned, but the old man kept complaining right up until Marisol scraped the front bumper against the curb parking in the back lot behind the bakery.

Leo's muscles relaxed. Next to her, Marisol let out a long sigh. Even the back seat went quiet long enough for Leo to breathe in the aroma of baking bread. For the first time since Abuela had woken her up, she felt safe.

"Where are we?" the old man asked.

With the strength of Amor y Azúcar surrounding her, Leo turned around in her seat.

"I'm really sorry I tricked you," she said. "My name is Leo Logroño, and my sister Marisol and I are brujas, and I accidentally brought you into the real world—well, we think I did, anyway, but it doesn't matter how you got here, because we're the ones who are going to help get you back. And I'm sorry about your garden. If you tell me where it is, maybe I can check on it for you?" The old man still looked suspicious, so Leo held out her hand as a peace offering.

The man shook it. "Well, it's nice to meet you

after all, Leo. Call me Old Jack. I suppose it was a bit mean to call you a con artist."

Leo nodded. "It's okay. You understand, though, don't you? Spirits aren't supposed to be in this world. I need to get all of you inside so my mom and my aunt can figure out what to do about this."

Old Jack shrugged. "I thought it was my chance to fix things," he said.

"I thought so too." Mrs. Morales patted his shoulder.

"But it wasn't," Abuela said. "It was just a mistake. Think of it as a joyride. We have to return the car eventually."

Old Jack crossed his arms. "Well, if that's the case, you shouldn't be worried about me and my little garden. You ought to go after the other man, the one who was heading to the school. He's probably making a lot more trouble than I am."

Oh no.

Leo felt Marisol's gasp like a candle flame held too close to her skin. Her face heated and her stomach dropped and even the smell of bread coming out of the oven couldn't make this okay. "There's another spirit?"

Old Jack nodded.

Marisol had parked between Daddy's truck and

Tía Paloma's old car, and suddenly Leo felt surrounded, facing disappointed faces on all sides.

She had no idea how these spirits had been set loose across the town. Was it really her magic? How many ghosts would appear? And if she couldn't stop them, what would happen to Leo, to her family, to Rose Hill?

She had picked the worst day in the world to fight with Caroline, because right now she wished more than anything that she could talk to her friend.

"I don't suppose it would do any good to ask you to *knock it off*, would it, cucaracha?" Marisol asked, her voice breathy and wobbling.

"I'm not doing anything," Leo replied, just as shaky. "I swear!"

Before the prickling in her throat could turn into full-blown sobs, Leo's worry was interrupted by a knock on her window. She turned around in her seat, terrified she'd see more orange flower petals.

Instead she saw Mamá, eyebrows raised and mouth opened wide, and that was enough to make the tears spill over.

CHAPTER 9

QUESTIONS AND ANSWERS

Inside the bakery, Mamá sat Leo on a stool and put a payaso cookie in her hand. She didn't *look* disappointed. The front of the bakery bustled with people picking up rosca de reyes orders and grabbing a couple of cookies or conchas and a coffee on their way out. This was the kind of rush Mamá always hoped for, but it made it hard to hide three spirits out of sight without causing a mess of dough and flour and bumping bodies in the kitchen.

"Isabel, the timers," Mamá called as alarms blared through the kitchen. She was keeping Abuela away from the bakery tables with one hand and pouring several cups of coffee with the other.

"I'm not going to ruin anything, Elena," Abuela complained. "I just want to see how it's going. It's my bakery, after all—let me look around."

"You have other things to focus on, Mami." Tía Paloma dragged Abuela to the corner by the cabinets. "I still don't understand how any of this is possible. Tell me what happened."

"Thank you, dear." Mrs. Morales accepted a cup of coffee, handed another to Old Jack, and let the twins lead her to a stool in front of the walk-in fridge.

"There's another spirit on the loose." Marisol tugged Mamá's sleeve, her voice high. "We don't even know if he's the last one. Where are they coming from?"

"Enough." Mamá shook Marisol off her arm. "I'm trying to understand too. Isabel, would you get the timers, *please*?"

Leo looked down at the pink, yellow, and white cookie in her hand. These were the ones Mamá spelled to put an extra-big smile on the face of little kids. She bit in, and sure enough, the bite danced in her mouth and down her throat, and she had to stifle giggles as a warm, bubbly feeling spread through her fingers and toes. Even if the happiness was artificial, it kept her from feeling too bad as Marisol explained her side of the story to Mamá—even when she suggested that it was Leo who had caused the whole mess.

"We tried to come straight here after getting the note from the Moraleses' house," Marisol said, "but we ran into this guy"—Old Jack nodded at Mamá with a smile—"and then he told us that there's another spirit too. And we need to go catch him, whoever he is, before someone realizes he's dead." Marisol gulped her coffee.

Mamá took a long breath, running a hand over her face. "Okay," she said. "I'll shut all the ovens off except the big one, and I'll tell Luis to start sending people away and lock the front door." Mamá peered toward the front of the bakery, where Daddy greeted another customer with a cheerful welcome. "We'll figure this out." She reached behind her back to undo the strings of her apron.

"Elena, no," Tía Paloma said. "It's so close to Día de Reyes, and we have more business than I've seen in years. We can't close down now."

Mamá scoffed. "I think this qualifies as an emergency situation. What do you want me to do? Sit here selling bread while my family needs me?"

"Your family needs you to stay calm and run your

business," Abuela said. "You have many capable bakers and brujas to help you, Maria Elena. You don't have to drop everything just to look after my old troublesome self."

"You always did for me," Mamá argued, even as she let Abuela retie the strings of her apron.

"And I expect you to do it for your children," Abuela said, patting Mamá's shoulder. "But me you don't worry about. Let Paloma and the girls take care of me for now. Keep the bakery running, and we'll be right here helping you out."

Mamá frowned. "My girls will help me out," she said. "You will stay well out of the way." Abuela nodded, holding up her hands and putting on her most innocent face. Mamá finally nodded. "All right. Paloma, can you use the scrying spell and see what information you can get about all this?" Another oven started to beep. "Isabel," Mamá called.

Isabel peeked her head in the door, twirling a thin sheet of waxed paper around a concha for a customer to carry home. "Sorry, I'm helping with the rush out here. And Daddy needs more change."

Mamá sent the twins to deal with the beeping oven, and Marisol scrambled to the office to break open rolls of quarters and dimes for the cash register.

Leo took another bite of her cookie as she watched

Tía Paloma pull a set of candles off a cabinet shelf and whisper to Abuela.

Marisol returned with grumpiness clouding her face. "Mamá, we're wasting time. I need to catch the spirit."

"We need all the facts," Mamá said. "We need to plan this out. You've been driving around after spirits all morning, and I don't want to send you out alone to chase another one with no idea where he could be. And I especially don't want to send Leo anywhere if it's indeed her power that's at play here."

"I don't need help," Marisol huffed, "and it wouldn't be with no idea, right?" She turned to Old Jack. "You know where the other spirit went?"

"He was headed toward the elementary school. Said something about teaching there when he was alive." Old Jack shrugged. "I couldn't hear everything he said at the time, but I have to say, I'm hearing much better now." He was looking a bit less hunched too, and his hair wasn't quite as thin as it had been. Leo had never heard of dead people (or any people) aging backward, and it made her nervous. "That was about a half hour ago. It's quite thrilling, isn't it, living every second? And I forgot how good coffee tastes too."

"Our bakery has the best coffee," Leo said softly

(even though it all tasted like burned socks to her).

"We need to get to the school," Marisol said. "Now. I can drive there."

Alma and Belén dropped a tray of swirly orejas on the nearest counter to cool and nodded their colorful heads in unison. "We should go too," Alma said.

"Yeah, you've been having all the excitement and we've just been lining up trays all morning," Belén complained.

"Except that if we're going to stay open, then I need you both here lining up trays—it's a very important job! And making dough and cutting cookies and icing the king cakes and . . ." Mamá shook her head. "Paloma, did the candles reveal anything?"

Tía Paloma looked up from her table, now filled with candles and herbs, and blinked. "I know they're not zombies."

Marisol groaned. "We figured that out hours ago."

Isabel rushed into the kitchen and joined Tía Paloma in her corner, switching one candle out for another and whispering furiously. The bell on the front door rang as more customers entered.

"We're a little shorthanded," Daddy's cheerful voice boomed from the other room, "but take your time looking around. Have you got your rosca de reyes yet? I'm sure we have a fresh batch coming out of the ovens any minute."

Leo stood up. "I can help with the register," she said. She was used to handling rushes, and Isabel would be more use in the back of the bakery anyway.

"Sit down, Leonora." Mamá's voice was sharp. "I want you to stay where I can see you. We've had quite enough surprises today."

Leo sat back on her stool and shoved the whole pink side of her triangle cookie into her mouth. *Useless.* Her family saw her as useless for anything but making a mess. She had to prove that she wasn't responsible for the spirits.

"On the back counter," Mamá corrected Alma, who was about to set a second tray of orejas to cool on the counter nearest the door, ready to be added to the shelves. "That's the special order."

"We're wasting time," Marisol told Mamá. "We need to catch the spirit at the school."

"School is out," Mamá argued calmly. "The building is empty. We can't spend the day chasing our tails all around town."

"But if someone sees him," Leo said. She could imagine one of the town busybodies catching sight of a strange man breaking into the closed school, calling the police. Marisol was right; they needed to catch him before someone else did.

"We need to focus on finding a solution," Mamá continued, barely glancing at Leo. "And we'll be better able to do that here, together."

"Or at home," Tía Paloma interrupted, leaving the corner to put a hand on Mamá's shoulder. "We're not having any luck revealing the nature of the spell here. Your very brilliant daughter"—Tía Paloma smiled at Isabel, who beamed—"thought that we might do better if we work with a location spell, from the place where the first spirit appeared. That was Leo's room, wasn't it?" She looked to Abuela for confirmation.

Abuela nodded. "I was pulled through into Leo's room, about seven in the morning."

"Seven in the morning?" Mrs. Morales, who had been enjoying her coffee so quietly that Leo had almost forgotten about her, spoke up. "But then you weren't the first spirit. I was pulled through hours before that." She hopped off her stool and joined the huddle near the front of the kitchen, marigold petals falling from her skirt with every step.

"Yes, I think I was pulled through at five in the morning, myself," Old Jack said. "I awoke with the dawn and the birds, and with a couple of terrible squirrels that have really made a mess of my old flower beds."

"Leti, why didn't you say anything earlier?" Abuela said.

"That changes things," Tía Paloma said softly, turning back to her corner.

"What does it mean?" Belén asked.

"It means that we really don't know what's going on." Worry creased Mamá's forehead.

Leo stood up off her stool. She felt restless energy tingling in her fingers. Her family was wasting time, like Marisol said. They were being just like they always were, busy and distracted and not paying Leo any attention, and the frustration of it all pressed against her skin like cinnamon sugar rolled deep into the layers of oreja dough. She shoved the last corner of the cookie into her mouth.

Usually, this was when she would talk to Caroline. But they stood in almost the same spot where Leo and her family had treated Caroline like an unwanted stranger yesterday. She was probably at home, not worrying about any magical disasters, just thinking about how angry she was at Leo. Maybe their friend Brent was visiting her house, and they were sitting on the trampoline making a plan to avoid Leo completely once school started back up. They would switch desks so Caroline didn't have to sit next to Leo. Maybe they would be seat buddies on the bus. They could even walk to school, if they wanted, to avoid Leo completely, because they lived so close—

Leo pressed her palms together as her brain caught up with itself. They lived so close to the school. . . .

"I know what to do," she said.

Tía Paloma stayed bent over her candles and herbs with Abuela. Mamá and Marisol traded trays as they loaded the ovens, and Isabel carried new treats to the front of the bakery. Alma and Belén conferred with each other as they wrapped the special orejas in individual sheets of wax paper.

"I know what to do!" Leo tried again. "You might not love it, but I think it will be the best—"

Isabel returned through the swinging doors, almost dropping the empty tray she carried as she crashed straight into Mrs. Morales, releasing another large cloud of orange petals. "Careful," Isabel hissed. "Someone could see you, or all of this!" She kicked orange petals off her shoe with a frown.

"Isabel Lucero, show some manners," Abuela snapped back.

Leo used the argument to drift farther back through the kitchen, passing Tía Paloma, who took no notice of the commotion.

"The reverse aging could be a factor," her aunt was mumbling. "Or it could simply have to do with their developing sense of their physical selves . . ." Her fingers twitched and then reached for one of her old books, flicking through the pages. "There must be an explanation . . . energy manifestation, maybe?"

Mrs. Morales's hair was totally black now, and both she and Abuela looked taller. Old Jack's head was filling up with more white hair.

Leo kept inching backward.

"We don't need babysitters," Mrs. Morales argued, pulling her elbow out of Isabel's grip.

"Then stop acting like babies!" Isabel whispered back.

In all the chaos, nobody noticed Leo slip into the office, pull the phone off Daddy's desk, and dial.

Caroline lived just a few minutes from the school. She already knew about magic. She might be mad, but Leo trusted her to help in an emergency. She was a good friend, and a good person. Leo didn't care if her sisters wouldn't approve. They needed help.

The phone rang once, twice.

"Leo?"

"Hi," Leo said. "I'm really sorry about yesterday."

"Oh, yeah . . . but don't be. I'm not—I've got some other things to—"

"Wait, listen." Leo gulped. "I really am sorry, and I know we need to talk, and I want to. But right now we have a big emergency, so that's why I called you. There are . . . ghosts. Well, they're spirits, really. They're coming into the real world, and they're running around town. They could cause really big problems if they are discovered; everyone in my family says so. If people know that spirits can come back to life, it will be a big mess. And we don't know exactly why they're here, but we think it has something to do with my magic. Well, everyone thinks it's my fault." Leo cringed. "But I don't think it is, and I need to prove it. And I would totally understand if you're sick of dealing with my magic problems, and if you hang up the phone right now, but if you aren't going to do that, then we could really use your help, because there's a spirit headed to the elementary school right now, and I thought maybe you could catch him faster than my family could."

The silence stretched, and Leo's stomach sank as she feared Caroline had hung up.

"What's his name?" Caroline finally said.

"Huh?"

"The ghost who was going to the school. The one you're looking for."

"Oh . . . I don't know." Leo tried to remember if

Old Jack had mentioned any details. "But you'll be able to recognize him because he'll leave a trail of flower petals behind him, orange ones. Old Jack, that's the ghost who told us about him, said they ran into each other and he said he was heading to the school—"

"Okay, good, hold on." Caroline pulled the phone away from her mouth and spoke in a loud but muffled voice. Leo didn't have time to worry who she was talking to before she returned. "Got it. That was Mr. Nguyen, you remember, from music. He ran into Mr. Jack an hour ago, and I caught him when he passed my house. He's one of the three I've got here. How many are at the bakery?"

For a moment, Leo wondered if someone had slipped a sleeping spell into her payaso cookie. Was this some strange dream? That somehow involved her elementary school music teacher? "You know about the ghosts?" she asked.

"Yes. How many do you have?"

"I . . . I have three. Abuela, and Mrs. Morales. And Old Jack."

Caroline let out a long sigh. "So that's six. Have any of your spirits mentioned any others?"

Leo tried to respond, but all that came out was a strangled squeak.

"Also, I don't think this is your fault," Caroline said.

"What do you mean?"

"I . . . have a confession to make."

Leo's mouth opened and closed while her brain sorted through Caroline's words.

Caroline knows about the spirits.

Caroline has spirits at her home.

Caroline doesn't think this is my fault.

"Leo," Caroline continued, "I think it was me."

"You?" Leo shook her head. "How is that possible?"

"I don't know, Leo," Caroline's voice rose to a squeak. "I don't know, and I'm kind of freaking out about it."

Slowly, like pouring honey, Leo worked out what she had to do.

"Don't move," Leo told her friend. "And don't worry. We're going to come help."

"Are you sure?" Caroline asked. "I'm not part of your family, or their magic."

"I'm sure." Leo would make her family listen. She would make them help Caroline. "We'll fix this." She balled her fists as she made the promise. "We're brujas. It's what we do."

She hung up the phone, stomped out of the office,

and planted her feet in the middle of the kitchen. "HEY!" she shouted above the beeping and whispering and laughing and grumbling. "Listen up, everyone!" Her face flushed as so many pairs of eyes turned toward her, looking surprised or confused or (in Marisol's case) annoyed. Leo cleared her throat. "We have to change our plans," she said. "I figured something out."

CHAPTER 10

CAROLINE'S HOUSE

With three brujas and three spirits, Mamá's van was stuffed like the walk-in fridge on milk and egg delivery day. Tía Paloma drove in her usual haphazard way, blinking owlishly at stop signs as she barreled through them and making as many wrong turns as right. She talked through her ideas for the location-based spell-revealing spell, half to herself and half to Isabel next to her.

Leo, seated in the second row of back seats, strained to hear their discussion.

"The revealing spell will confirm if the spirits really originated from something Caroline did,"

Isabel said. "I'm still not so sure Leo didn't have something to do with it."

Leo tried to protest, but of course no one paid attention.

"You might be right, but even so, the spirits are gathering in that house. It must be relevant somehow. And even if we just get a glimpse of the original spell, that will make it much easier to cook up an unraveling spell." Tía Paloma slammed on the brakes, and all the passengers jolted forward.

Leo had used an unraveling spell to reverse the effects of a problematic spell once before. They were tricky to get right because you had to use ingredients that were the magical opposites of those used in the original spell. Leo tapped her feet against the floor of the van and hoped that the revealing spell turned up useful information. She would be terrified to try to reverse a spell when she didn't even know what the original spell was.

Isabel, though, grinned. Magical theory was her favorite aspect of being a bruja. "We've never seen anything like this before."

"For good reason," Tía Paloma warned, her voice sober. "This isn't a game, Isabel. Whatever Leo or Caroline are messing with, it's dangerous."

"I know." Isabel's voice lost its sparkle. "I didn't

mean . . . This never would have happened if Leo hadn't been doing so much magic with Caroline."

Leo sat back against her seat angrily. She was tired of being blamed for everything, tired of Isabel's rudeness toward her friend. She turned her face to the rain-sprinkled window, no longer interested in hearing the magical shop talk. In the first row of back seats, Abuela and Mrs. Morales fought for elbow room and joked about when they were young. Old Jack leaned against the window next to them and sighed every time they passed a particularly nice garden.

As her mind began to wander, Leo thought she saw something shimmer in front of the window, like a piece of plastic wrap covering the glass. She reached for it, but when she moved her hand toward the window, it blurred and rippled. Before she could figure out what it was, they were pulling onto Caroline's street. It was still and silent, and they found her driveway empty. The oleander bushes on either side of her door didn't even rustle in the breeze. Leo climbed over the back seat and tumbled out to stand on the wet lawn with Tía Paloma, Isabel, Abuela, and the other spirits.

"Oh yes," Abuela whispered, breaking the hush. "This is where it started. I can feel it."

Mrs. Morales nodded, giving an exaggerated shiver and spraying flower petals into Leo's face.

"What does that mean?" Leo asked Isabel in a low voice, but Isabel busied herself taking Tía Paloma's books out of the van, arranging the stack neatly in her arms in size order, and adjusting the purse across her shoulder.

Leo huffed out an angry breath and marched up to the front door. She tried sniffing the air, but she only smelled the sharp smell of wet grass and dirt and oleander. No spice. "I don't feel anything," she muttered.

But when she rang the doorbell and faced the frosted-glass panel of Caroline's door, the white window seemed to shimmer with a shiny film, just as the one in the car had. Was this the power Abuela felt? Leo rubbed her eyes until Caroline's face appeared in the doorway.

"Leo!" Caroline opened the door only a crack, poked her head out, and glanced up and down the street. "I'm so glad you're here. Things are getting hectic, and I'm sorry I didn't call you earlier, but it's really scary and I don't know what to do. Oh." Isabel walked up behind Leo, and Caroline ducked to hide her eyes behind her bangs. "Hi, Isabel."

"Caroline." Isabel matched Caroline's cold voice.

Leo stifled a groan. She didn't have time to figure out how to fix things between her sister and her friend. "Shouldn't we get the spirits inside?" she reminded them.

Leo hadn't seen the Campbells' living room so loud and busy since before Mrs. Campbell got sick. There was Mr. Nguyen, who had taught music at Rose Hill Elementary until Leo was in fourth grade. Even though he was a spirit, Leo grinned when she saw the familiar glasses and gray hair—he had always been one of her favorite teachers. She smiled and waved.

Beside him was a pale man with a long gray beard, big-toothed smile, and thick hair slicked to one side like Daddy when he was getting dressed for church. And there was also a tall, muscular middle-aged man with tattoos peeking out of the sleeves of his leather jacket and over the collar of his blue T-shirt.

Leo raised her eyebrows. Her morning had been stressful, frustrating, and confusing, but at least she hadn't had to deal with a group of strange grown-ups all on her own. She felt extra impressed with Caroline, and extra happy that her family was here now, ready to help banish the spirits for good.

"Miguel Antonio Pérez!" Abuela's voice and laugh

cut over the general chatter of six ghosts and four humans. "Is that really you?"

Mrs. Morales tugged Abuela's sleeve, looking embarrassed, but Abuela ignored her. "You really grew into that height, didn't you? I haven't seen you in years! Long before I died, I mean."

The muscled, tattooed man clomped over to Abuela in boots Marisol would envy. He grinned and clapped Abuela into a hug, then held his arms open for Mrs. Morales.

"Lucy and Leti, you're both looking beautiful as ever. Tell me you weren't this young when you stretched up your paws?" He frowned. "Huh. It's convenient to be able to speak in English easily now, but some things really don't sound as good."

Mrs. Morales looked about three inches shorter than usual, but she gave the man a quick hug and kissed his cheek. "No, Miguel Antonio," she said, "some of us had enough sense to avoid those terrible motorcycles and got to see our old age." She frowned at him, and hit the shoulder of his leather jacket lightly. "You upset your family, you know. Ratoncito."

"Ah, Leti, I know. I owe them an apology." The man, Mr. Pérez, shrugged his big shoulders. "So that's why you married Alfredo and not me, right?"

For a second, Mrs. Morales looked like she had taken a big sip of milk only to find it sour. But then her face relaxed and she clicked her tongue at the big man. “Sinvergüenza,” she muttered, loud enough for him to hear and chuckle.

Meanwhile, the older man made his way around the room, shaking hands with Tía Paloma and Isabel and Old Jack before reaching the corner of the couch where Leo and Caroline stood.

“Abraham Rose,” he announced. “Former mayor of Rose Hill. I was around back when Rose Hill was nothing more than unincorporated territory.” He winked at Leo. “And look how we’ve grown.” He swept his hands in a circle as if the whole town could be seen through the closed blinds of the living room.

The bustle was starting to remind Leo of Easter gatherings with the Logroño side of the family, with her aunts and uncles and cousins who normally lived across the state all packed into one house for the weekend and usually fighting with each other in between mouthfuls of chocolate. She stepped back to put more of the couch between her and the spirits, catching Caroline’s eye as she did.

“There’s a lot going on,” Caroline said, scooting into the corner next to Leo. She gave an apologetic shrug. “I’m glad you’re here.”

Leo smiled and returned the shrug. "Me too," she said. "I thought my magic was malfunctioning again."

Caroline wrapped her arms around her stomach. "How do we fix this? I don't even know what's happening."

"That's what we're here to figure out." Tía Paloma squeezed around Miguel Antonio's broad frame to join the two girls in their corner. "But we can't get started without more information. Is there a quieter place we can sit and talk through this?"

Caroline glanced at the spirits as Isabel nodded her way out of another handshake from Mayor Rose. "I'm not sure about leaving them alone," she admitted. "Mr. Pérez tried to sneak out the back door twice already to find his sister, and the mayor won't stop talking about getting over to city hall to register as a candidate in the next election."

"I know just how to get the town back on track," Mayor Rose interjected, his head swiveling as soon as he heard Caroline mention him. "I'll put us back on the map. I just need to fill out the paperwork before the deadline."

Caroline rolled her eyes and snorted, but Leo didn't think the idea of a dead mayor walking into city hall was very funny. Isabel kept her face calm, but by the way she smoothed the front of her skirt and then twisted her hands together, Leo guessed she wasn't amused either.

"If this guy is running for mayor, I don't see why I can't pull a few weeds in my garden," Old Jack grumbled.

"Or why I can't go tune the school piano," Mr. Nguyen added. "Mr. Song has no idea how to treat it. He got rid of my dehumidifier; he never puts the cover on it at the end of the school day. . . . I didn't leave my Steinway to the school for a whole generation of music students to be singing flat Cs and sharp Es."

"I can't hear myself think." Tía Paloma sighed. "This is too much ghost chatter, even for me."

"Actually . . ." Isabel smoothed her already wrinkle-free skirt again. "I have a way to help with that part. If we want to talk privately." She opened the round black purse hanging from her shoulder and pulled out a bundle twisted in wax paper, with two lumps on top and a smooth circular bottom. Tía Paloma clapped her hands and nodded when she saw it.

"Is that a listening oreja?" Leo asked. She had seen her sisters make batches of those rolled-up pastries, spelled to make whoever ate them into a better listener. The recipe in the family spell book called for the bruja to listen to two sides of an argument while rolling butter into the pastry dough. Mamá and Marisol had helped Isabel with that part.

"'Share a bite with a friend or an enemy, and soon you'll be able to hear each other without impediments or distractions.'" Isabel quoted the family spell book from memory. "It's usually used for emotional distractions, like when someone is too upset to listen, but it can work in lots of ways. I knew a Spanish speaker who used to use them to communicate better with her English-speaking coworkers. It didn't change their languages, but it helped everyone try harder to understand, even when it wasn't easy." Isabel broke the oreja into four pieces, keeping one for herself and handing the others to Leo, Caroline, and Tía Paloma. "So let's get rid of some of the impediments to our conversation."

Leo brought her piece to her mouth, holding one hand under her chin to catch the thin crumbs that flaked off when she bit down. She tasted cinnamon sugar and buttery bread and the whiff of magic. Then, like a song fading out on the radio, the noise of Abuela laughing and Mrs. Morales scolding Mr. Pérez began to fade, along with Old Jack's grumbling, Mayor Rose's campaign speech, and Mr.

Nguyen's humming. Although the spirits were still in the room, Leo hardly noticed them anymore.

Caroline and Isabel let out twin sighs of relief.

"That's much better," Tía Paloma said. "Very good thinking, Isabel, bringing that along. I wasn't even imagining such a commotion. Now I think we should start from the beginning with—"

"Wait," Isabel said. "I have something I want to say first. It's the reason I brought the oreja. I actually wasn't expecting anything like this." She gestured at the spirits.

Leo nodded, leaning toward Isabel instinctively as she waited for her sister to continue.

"I . . . well, I wanted to talk to you, Caroline." Isabel ran her hands down her skirt once more and cleared her throat. "I wanted to apologize for . . . maybe not acting very friendly toward you yesterday at the bakery. Whenever you're at the bakery, actually."

Was it the oreja making Leo think she could hear a world of feelings behind Isabel's words? As she wondered this, she thought of what Marisol had said, about Isabel not having any close friends from school, or from anywhere, and that she spent most of her time talking to Mamá or Tía Paloma or the Logroño cousins that were her age. She understood how Isabel might feel left out when Marisol went to parties with kids from Rose Hill High, parties with kids who were seniors like Isabel, and how that feeling of loneliness could have come out unfairly as resentment toward Leo and her friend. She remembered that Isabel hated breaking any rule or disappointing Mamá in any way—but that she had been the one to disobey tradition by telling Leo about the family magic just a few months ago, because she didn't want Leo to feel lonely or left out anymore. And instead of keeping her sister's secret, Leo had blabbed to Caroline and then made a huge mess of two spells, trying to fix Caroline's friendship with Brent.

Maybe Isabel shouldn't have taken all those feelings out on Caroline yesterday, but it did sort of make sense now.

"Thank you," Caroline said. "I wasn't trying to be annoying, hanging around so much, but I can see how it might be frustrating when everyone is so busy. I just like the bakery. I don't want you all to hate me."

Caroline didn't have any sisters or brothers, and her family was all far away and separated by borders and language—and grief, now, after her mother had passed away. Naturally, she would like to sit by the cash register with Leo and pretend to belong in the easy routine of the bakery. It wasn't the spells that drew her to help Leo study; she wasn't trying to figure out Logroño family secrets like Leo had been last year, or looking for magical shortcuts to solve all her problems. She just wanted to be near the true magic of the Logroño family—their love and closeness.

"We don't hate you," Isabel said as she put her hand on the younger girl's shoulder. "How could we hate someone who is so important to our favorite littlest sister?"

Caroline's smile was small, and watery, but it was there. And Leo smiled as well.

"I'm glad you girls could work this out," Tía Paloma said. "And I want you to know that as far as I'm concerned, you're welcome at the bakery anytime, Caroline." Her smile was sincere. "Now, while we have a moment of peace and quiet, do you mind telling us how you think all the spirits came to be here?"

It was a little scary for Leo, hearing the confusion in her aunt's words—the most expert bruja she knew was completely baffled. But she also felt less alone. It was going to take all of them to fix this, and Leo was confident they could.

"Okay," Caroline said, her eyes cast down and her cheeks pink. She was embarrassed, confused, and scared—exactly how Leo remembered feeling all the times her spells had ended up wrong. "Here's what happened."

CHAPTER 11
STORIES

"When I was in Costa Rica," Caroline said, "I felt really . . . I missed my mom a lot."

Caroline had said something similar when she had come to the bakery the day before, but Leo hadn't really been listening then. Her ears turned hot. She shouldn't need a magic spell to listen to her friend. Just this weekend had been strange without Mamá in the bakery, everything changing and shifting to make up for her absence. She couldn't imagine how much worse it would feel for Caroline to travel without her mother, how hard that trip would be.

"I guess I never realized that I'm so American. When I was with my mom, she would talk to everyone in the airport and in the stores and everything, and she made Costa Rica feel like home. But without her it just . . . didn't. It all changed too."

Leo thought about how Caroline and her dad had rearranged and redecorated their whole house in the past few months. They had wanted things to be different, to reflect the truth that nothing would ever feel the same. But it seemed hard to face heartache without a familiar place to sleep.

"My family was nice, but I felt disconnected. Like, without my mom I'm not really part of the family. And then I tried calling Leo when I came back, but she could never talk, and so I went to the bakery, but everyone acted like I shouldn't be there either. It's just for your family. And I got mad. So I . . . I'm sorry. I shouldn't have done it. But I stole a candle."

Tía Paloma nodded with a heavy sigh. "Belén's candle."

Caroline nodded. "I don't know why I did it. But once I got home, I was thinking about how my grandmother has veladoras burning in her house, and how they're supposed to be like prayers that keep going all the time. As long as the candle stays lit, it's like someone's still listening. And I wanted . . . that.

I wanted Mom to be listening."

"So you lit a candle for the dead." Isabel nodded. "Of course you did. And with all your deep feelings poured into it, and the fact that it already had Belén's spirit magic running through it . . ."

There was a long silence, and Leo wondered if the whisper in her head was Caroline's thought or her own, or if everyone was thinking the same thing she was thinking, her eyes flickering across the six spirits in the room. Could Caroline's action really have caused so many spirits to return from the dead?

"Caroline," Tía Paloma said, her voice gentle, "this is very important. Does your family have any history of brujería? I admit it's possible that what you did could have caused this, but in all my years I've never heard of such a powerful result with just a relic and some secondhand magical knowledge. If we have a second strain of witchcraft built into this spell, then it's going to be extra complicated to unravel. We need to know as much as we can."

"I don't know," Caroline said, and Leo could hear the truth in her words even without the oreja's magic.

Tía Paloma sighed through her nose, her lips shut tight. But before she could say any more, Isabel said, "That's okay." Her hand landed protectively on Caroline's shoulder again. "We can recast the revealing spell, and maybe that will help us. Where is the candle?"

"In my room," Caroline answered, "on my bedside table."

"See?" Isabel said. "You probably had other objects on your bedside table, right? An altar you didn't even know you were making. That helps already; we can use those to help us make a reverse spell. Let's go see it."

"But what about all the ghosts?" Caroline said.

"Spirits," Leo said. Most of them were sitting and talking animatedly about finding their loved ones, and Mr. Pérez paced restlessly, as if getting ready to make a run for it.

"Leo," Tía Paloma said, "keep an eye on them. Distract them. We need to figure out the spell. Please?"

Isabel smiled encouragingly at Leo and walked Caroline into the hallway and through her butterfly-painted bedroom door. Caroline shot one apologetic glance over her shoulder before Tía Paloma shut the door behind her. Leo felt the oreja spell snap like a rubber band as the conversation left her, and the raised voices of the spirits resumed their normal volume.

Leo sighed. She couldn't be mad at Caroline for

getting caught up in the excitement of magical secrets and leaving Leo behind, not when she had done the same thing to her friend. And she couldn't be mad at Tía Paloma or Isabel, who had given her a useful job that would help them focus on their investigation. She couldn't even be mad at the spirits, who were as confused by this as anyone else. So instead, all her anger sat in her stomach like a lump of undigested oatmeal, weighing her down. She sighed again. How was she supposed to keep six spirits busy and happy and distracted from trying to leave the house for as long as it took her family to figure out the spell?

"Hey," she said in her loudest fighting-with-Marisol voice. "Hey, listen up, everybody!"

Six pairs of eyes flicked her way.

"Who's hungry?"

She made coffee first (tea for Mayor Rose), taking the six orders of cream and sugar and working out the small mysteries of the Campbells' coffee machine while the spirits grumbled their way into the kitchen. Leo's experience handling the cash register during the morning rush at the bakery made this small stampede easy enough to handle.

Once everyone was settled with a warm mug, she opened the refrigerator to see what kind of breakfast she could throw together. The refrigerator was in good shape, filled with healthy food and no prepeeled boiled eggs, but making something would require more cooking skill than Leo felt she had. She understood the huge ovens of Amor y Azúcar well enough to change out trays or set a timer, but she wasn't quite as confident with a family-sized stove. So in the end, she pulled two Toaster Strudel boxes out of the freezer.

"This is not in keeping with the traditions of our family," Abuela grumbled as Leo popped the pastries out of the toaster and onto plates two at a time and Mrs. Morales squeezed a packet of sugar icing in a squiggly trail across them. "It's not even strudel," she moaned, pinching the crispy dough between her fingers.

Biting into the last pastry from the second box, Leo had to agree with Abuela. She would take one of Mamá's guava-and-cheese conos over the super-sweet store-bought treats any day. Still, the spirits ate quietly and sipped their coffee without complaint, so there must have been some magic, even in Toaster Strudel.

"May I have another?" Mr. Pérez asked politely.

There was a third box in the freezer, but Leo wondered if Mr. Campbell would get suspicious if it seemed like Caroline had gone through eighteen breakfast snacks in one day. She held up a finger to Mr. Pérez and then ducked back toward the hallway to ask Caroline.

Caroline wasn't in her room anymore. Instead, she stood in the middle of the hall, giving Tía Paloma instruction as she tugged down the trapdoor in the ceiling to release a folded ladder up to the attic.

"What's going on?" Leo asked.

"Something weird." Caroline held out her hand to show Leo a silvery Monopoly game piece (the iron), a red Sorry! token, and a hexagonal piece of cardboard with a flat miniature forest painted on it from Settlers of Catan. "These appeared on my bedside table."

Leo prodded the iron. "You mean, when you all tried to perform the reveal spell?"

"No," Caroline said. "They were there when we went into the room. And the board games they belong to are all packed up in the attic!"

"Wow," Leo's voice dropped low to match Caroline's. "That is weird. So, you're going to investigate?"

"I guess so." Caroline's smile looked frazzled. "We're still looking for clues. Your aunt says I must have powers of my own, which is so weird. But did you need something?"

"No, it's fine." Leo couldn't help but smile. Sometime, when the mysteries were solved and the spirits restored to el Otro Lado, when Caroline had time to hear it, she would tell her friend how excited she was to have a friend with magic, how much fun they could have together learning more about their powers. For now, though, she just gave her friend a thumbs-up. "Good luck."

Tía Paloma waved Caroline onto the ladder, and Leo left as her friend climbed up to see what magical mysteries hid in her attic. She made her way back to the kitchen, skipping in excitement.

The spirits had finished the last box of toaster pastries on their own and were now helping themselves to a family-sized box of shredded wheat. Leo brushed away a pile of orange petals and sat on the counter, her brain buzzing over Caroline's magic—she had real magic!—and what it meant. Did Caroline have a birth-order power? Would she have to develop a family skill to channel her magic, the way the Logroños had with baking? What if her family had a boring aptitude, like being able to magically fill out tax forms?

Leo's brain swirled through ideas like milk swirling at the bottom of Abuela's empty cereal bowl, and her fingers tapped a line down the Campbells' counter. She should have learned more about other people's magic. She should have asked Isabel more about the spellcraft convention, or read some of Tía Paloma's books.

Tía Paloma's spell books, or most of them, at least, still sat in a stack on the counter where Isabel had dropped them. Some were old and bound in leather with handwritten pages, like the family book of magical recipes Leo had stolen out of the bakery last year. Others were thin and new, with plain-colored covers. Only one of them was in English, and as she skimmed through the chapter titles, it seemed to deal mostly with crystals and wildflowers, with only a small section on "Candles and Summoning." Leo was about to set the book aside and try to tackle one of the Spanish ones—*Curanderismo y brujería en las Americas* sounded promising if she wanted to learn about other types of magic—when she noticed one of Tía Paloma's saint cards bookmarking a page in the English book. She flipped the thin pages to where San Pascual peeked out at her, and read:

The summoning of deceased spirits or otherworldly beings may be achieved by certain practitioners, especially those with an inherited capacity for it, using one or more candles and a good deal of will. Anything from an unexplained breeze to a brief sensory interaction with the summoned entity may indicate success.

Leo glanced up from the page. She watched Abuela pour herself more coffee, yawning as she upended the mostly empty pot. These spirits were a lot more than an unexplained breeze or a brief interaction. She stood to help Abuela make more coffee and bumped elbows with her grandmother. Abuela was a lasting, five-senses apparition. Why had Caroline's spell been so powerful?

"It's exhausting, isn't it?" Mrs. Morales asked Abuela, taking a long sip from her own mug. "Being in the living world?"

"I forgot how hard it was to move with a body," Mr. Pérez said, nodding. "And right that it's weird to have skin?" He pinched his cheeks and pulled his face in opposite directions, making Abuela and Mrs. Morales giggle. When he dropped his hands, he traced the cursive letters of a tattoo that circled his wrist. "It is strange how I forgot about it. You have to hold yourself together and keep everything else out. It takes so much energy. How did we manage it for so many years?"

"Well, that's why we got old." Abuela laughed. "And ugly."

"Speak for yourself, viejita," Mrs. Morales declared with a flourish of her skirt.

But she was wrong. Abuela didn't look so old anymore. Her body had straightened and smoothed considerably since she had first appeared by Leo's bed, and her movements looked surer. Her face was more round, her hair dark and thick where it swept back from her forehead into its bun. She looked more like Mamá than the abuela Leo remembered—all except for her eyes, dark brown-black and full of grumbly humor as she joked with her friends. Her eyes were the same, even if the rest of her was getting younger every minute.

Leo picked the book back off the counter and scanned the page, an uneasy feeling nagging at the back of her brain. Her eyes flicked over paragraphs detailing specific types of candles and their uses, and she felt frustration tighten her throat even though she wasn't sure what exactly she was looking for.

Finally she saw, at the bottom of the page, a single line among the many tiny numbered footnotes. "For more on the effects of summoning the deceased, see Appendix IV."

Leo silently thanked Ms. Luchesi, her school librarian, for teaching proper research skills as she flipped to the table of contents and then the correct page.

She read the whole section, then started over and read it again. She took a long breath.

"Abuela," she said. Her voice barely made a sound over the fear stuck in her throat. "Can you come look?"

"What's wrong, Leonora?" Abuela leaned over her shoulder.

"What are you reading?" Mrs. Morales leaned on Leo's other side and inspected the book.

A tiny voice in Leo's head whispered to her to flip the book shut, to lie, to hope she had read everything all wrong. But more secrets and denial weren't going to help anything, and tricks couldn't get her out of this problem.

She pointed to the paragraph in question. "Does this mean what I think it means?"

Appendix IV described a sorceress, Elisheva Zafrani, who was able to send letters to her husband after her death.

By following her instructions, he was able to summon her spirit even though he possessed no magic himself—he was even able to help her achieve an inconsistent visual manifestation. Zafrani's letters, though, show the toll that these repeated manifestations took on her spirit. She describes feeling "drained" and "uncomfortable" in this world, and chides her husband for complimenting her appearance. "You say I grow more beautiful with every passing day, full of youth, as if I have shed my years. But it is myself, not my age, which I lose. My love, you must not call me again, or I am sure I shall lose myself in this empty realm of the living and never find my way back to peace." Her fears echo a commonly cited wisdom, that bringing spirits into our world too often, or for too long, can cause them to disintegrate, becoming tortured and haunting fragments of their former selves.

Abuela bit her lip. She lifted the book and pulled it closer to her face, tilting it away from Mrs. Morales. "¿Qué diablos?" she whispered. Her mouth moved silently as her finger dragged over the same lines over and over. Leo had focused on just one word.

Disintegrate.

The age spots on the backs of Abuela's hands had

almost faded away, veins hidden under stronger skin. By normal living-person standards, she looked strong and healthy. But Leo missed the fingers twisted with arthritis and creased from decades of life.

"It's bad, right?" Leo asked, putting a hand over Abuela's to stop her rereading.

Abuela looked up from the paper, her bottomless-pit eyes fierce and frightening. "Hush, Leo. Don't say anything yet. We don't want to spook . . ." Her eyes flicked to Mr. Pérez, who stared moodily out the window while sipping his coffee, and Mayor Rose, who had started a conversation with Old Jack that was half whispers and half requests for the mayor to "Speak up, sir!"

Leo nodded. She needed to think, and she needed to find out if this was true, and she needed to do it without causing a panic among the spirits in Caroline's kitchen. She tugged the end of her braid. "Maybe I should . . ." She glanced toward the hall where Tía Paloma, Isabel, and Caroline were still exploring the attic.

Mrs. Morales put an arm around Abuela's shoulders. "Go ahead, tell your aunt what's happening. Hurry." She waved her arm to shoo Leo.

Leo nodded, hesitated, and then followed Mrs.

Morales's flapping arm and dancing marigold petals out of the kitchen.

"Caroline?" she whispered from the bottom of the attic steps. "Caroline, are you up there?"

A draft of air from the attic hit her face, warm and dusty and carrying the scent of old paper. As she blinked against the breeze, the space in front of the ladder seemed to shimmer and wave like a curtain following the current of air—just like she'd seen earlier on the car window and outside Caroline's door. Leo blinked until the effect faded.

"Leo." Caroline's head appeared in the rectangular hole in the ceiling, her eyes gleaming but her voice hushed. "Is that you? We found something." She pulled her head back, and a second later her fuzzy green slipper socks poked out of the dark ceiling and landed on the top step of the ladder. "We found something that might help!"

Leo opened her mouth to explain the fear squeezing around her chest, but then closed it. If Caroline had discovered how to send the spirits back, then there was no need to worry about what would happen to them if they stayed. She let out a shaky breath.

As Caroline's flannel pajama shorts and button-down shirt descended from the attic, Leo caught sight of a gray-brown journal, about the size of a postcard and thinner than a pack of playing cards. Caroline cradled it to her chest with one hand while the other held the thin railing to guide her down to the hallway floor.

Leo bounced on her toes. "Is that your spell book?" she blurted out. "Does it belong to your family? Can you use it to send the spirits home?"

Caroline shook her head, hugging the book to her chest. "It's just my great-grandmother's diary. My mom kept it in her treasure box, but I couldn't read it when I was younger."

Leo had seen Mrs. Campbell's treasure box once, when Caroline brought it to school for show and tell. It was light brown with a latched lid, made of some kind of wood that left its smell on the treasures inside—a crystal-beaded rosary, library cards from every library Mrs. Campbell had ever worked at, report cards from her lower school in Costa Rica. Leo didn't remember seeing the small book inside, but maybe her eyes had danced over it, too intrigued by the miniature domino set or the handmade paper dolls. Maybe Mrs. Campbell had removed the book from the box before sending it to school, or maybe the book had hidden itself because it really was magic.

"Can you read it now?" Leo's curiosity combined with the worry of her finger stuck between the pages of the appendix, resting on the word "disintegrate." She hopped up and down. "Does it say anything about sending them back to el Otro Lado?"

Caroline shook her head. "It's not like that, Leo. She tells some stories about her aunt and uncle, and about our family history—she mentions that generations back, her great-grandparents were both curanderos, and they healed people's illnesses and injuries and helped them with their problems. There are notes about using candles for magical healing, not all that different from what Tía Paloma has been teaching you and your sisters. So I guess there is magic in my family. I think there's more to it, because she said that our focus shifted, but I don't know to what. I'm going to keep reading, because your aunt says that knowing more specifics about my . . . about the magic that brought the spirits here will help with, um, something?" Caroline shrugged.

"It will help us devise an unraveling spell." Tía Paloma climbed down the ladder slowly, her hands gripping the handrail tightly and her feet flailing through the air with each step down. She landed with an "oof" on the hallway floor. "I want to look more closely, of course, but we have two good clues from that paragraph you read: that your magic is rooted in curanderismo, and that your family regularly channeled magic through candles. Those are great places to start."

Leo frowned. Those might be good places to start, but they didn't sound like an answer that could be used to send the spirits home—not yet. She tapped the thin cover of the book she was holding and opened her mouth, but the bad news stuck on her tongue, and before she could free it, another voice interrupted.

"I want to take a look at your altar again too," Isabel said as she descended the ladder with one hand holding her skirt close to her legs. "I'm imagining that we'll make a separate one for the unraveling, probably more intricate to deal with the fact that your spell combined our family magic on the candle with your family magic. But we can still try to use similar elements, or ones that are symbolically opposite. . . ." She reached the floor and turned to face the group. "Leo! What are you doing here?"

"I came to tell you," Leo whispered, "that I was looking through some of the books you left in the living room and . . . I found something. Something . . . maybe bad. How soon until we have an unraveling spell, do you think?"

Isabel frowned. "This is a complicated situation, and we still don't have all the information yet. It's going to take hours—at least—to come up with even a basic outline."

Leo winced. "Okay," she said. "That's not good." She held out the book, opened to the appendix.

Before anyone could look, though, the sound of a door slamming shut startled them all. Caroline spun around. Tía Paloma's eyes, magnified by her glasses, bulged like a frog's. Isabel looked at Leo, eyebrows spiking up her forehead.

"Leo, you left the spirits alone, didn't you?"

CHAPTER 12

CRY FOR HELP

Caroline bolted for the kitchen, and Leo was right behind her, ears ringing with her sister's words. She banged her shin against the coffee table, barely registering the pain as her mind hoped that somehow this was all a silly misunderstanding and the spirits would be sitting at the table eating Toaster Strudel when she arrived.

By the time Leo skidded to a stop on the linoleum kitchen floor, Caroline was already there, shaking her head slowly back and forth. "They're gone."

Leo yanked open the back door. "Come on," she said, "We have to catch them!"

Isabel and Tía Paloma stayed in the kitchen doorway, faces tight and worried. "Do you see them?" Isabel asked.

Leo shook her head.

"I think running down the block after them would look more suspicious," Tía Paloma said. "The last thing we want is to cause a scene."

Leo stared at the kitchen table, still ringed by seven empty mugs and one half-eaten bowl of shredded wheat. She traced the trail of petals out the back door and down the driveway, where it scattered in multiple windswept directions. Fear settled into its familiar spot at the bottom of her stomach, spreading out all its wiggly tentacles and shoving her breakfast into a lump as it made itself comfortable.

Where were the spirits going to go? How could they avoid a scene while all six of them were running around town?

"You were supposed to be watching them." Isabel spoke the accusation softly, but Leo wanted to cover her ears. Isabel tugged the hem of her shirt and smoothed her skirt, fingers picking away viciously at invisible spots of lint.

"Settle, Isabel." Tía Paloma held out a hand. "Leo? I don't understand. You just turned your back for a minute and they all decided to run away? That doesn't make sense." She stared out the kitchen window at the trail.

It's not my fault, Leo wanted to say, except this time even the thought felt like a lie. She wanted to say, *I'm sorry.*

"I know why they left," she said instead. "I was about to tell you." She freed her finger from the thin magic book and spread it open on the counter. "I think the spirits are in danger."

"Danger? What kind?" Isabel leaned to read the book, but Tía Paloma snatched it away first, her fingers skimming down the page until she slammed the book back onto the counter.

"Of course." She sighed. "You had that hunch, Isabel. Their energy is being depleted by being here. So if we don't get them back, they'll—"

"Disintegrate," Leo said. The world sounded even scarier spoken aloud.

Tía Paloma pursed her lips. "Did you tell them about this, Leo?"

"No!" Leo hunched her shoulders, cheeks burning. "I mean . . . just Abuela. And Mrs. Morales saw the page too. But they're the ones who told me not to tell anyone, and to go get you so you could—"

Oh. Mrs. Morales had sent her away on purpose, and she had fallen for it. She hugged her arms across her stomach, where the fear tentacles mixed with embarrassment. It wasn't so much fun to be on this side of tricking people into doing what you wanted.

"I don't get it," Caroline said. She was looking at the book. "It sounds like they're going to . . . die?" Her forehead wrinkled. "But they're already dead."

"They'll lose themselves." Isabel spoke quietly. She reached for the book and flipped the pages, lifting it to her face and scanning. "They won't be able to hold themselves together anymore, so they'll break into pieces. Become nothing."

"Everything," Leo corrected, remembering how Abuela had described el Otro Lado. "She said they become everything. But it didn't sound like a bad thing."

"And in el Otro Lado, it's not." Abuela appeared at the open back door, her eyes tired and her steps heavy. "But on this side of the veil, it's a different story." Her eyes fell. "I'm sorry. I tried to stop them. But that mayor went and gave a rousing speech, and it turns out I'm not much good at convincing people when I can't use my influence."

"What did the mayor say?" Caroline asked. "What do they want?"

"If this is about running out of energy and disintegrating, shouldn't they stay here instead of tiring themselves out around the city?" Isabel added.

Abuela sat heavily at the kitchen table. "They're afraid," she said. "Miguel Antonio wants to go apologize to his sister, and that teacher wants to tend to his piano, and so on. They know they're running out of time, and the mayor stirred them up asking how they would want to spend their last hours before they . . ." Abuela waved her hands in the air and fluttered a few petals into a coffee mug. "Poof. Into nothing, like dust. We'll be real ghosts then, the kind that are lost. Broken, like La Llorona." Leo offered Abuela a fresh cup of coffee and got a weary smile in return. Abuela cupped the warm mug in both hands and took a sip before she continued.

"In el Otro Lado, you can flow like water. Be yourself, or not yourself, just following the current and drifting in the possibilities. El Otro Lado is where magic operates, where objects can be drawn out of thin air and where emotions take shape and form and can be altered. Where spirits walk and talk and stay safe." She shook her head. "Without the magic to protect us, we'll fade and scatter, and then we won't be able to find our way back to ourselves. Or any of the things and people we love."

"That's horrible." Isabel sank into a chair next to Abuela, reaching for her grandmother's hand and clinging tightly to it.

"We'll have to unravel the spell," Tía Paloma said, voice thick as she hid her face behind the book she had returned to reading. "As soon as possible."

"We have to find the spirits," Leo said. Their escape might put them in more danger by speeding up the process of disintegration, but it also put them in danger of being caught. Since she had let them escape, any confusion or chaos they caused to the town—or to her family, by giving away their secret—was her fault.

"I have to read this." Caroline held up her diary from the attic. "I need to know more about my family magic. I need to understand what I did."

Leo nodded. "You need Tía Paloma to help you, and Isabel," she said. "So it's up to me to go after the spirits."

She puffed out her chest, waiting for the arguments to come. *You're too young, too small, you'll make a mess of it. Leave it to someone else, Little Leo. Don't worry about it.* She wasn't going to accept it, wasn't going to sit back and watch everyone else be part of the solution while she sat on the sidelines. Not anymore.

"Of course," Isabel said. "That makes sense."

"Thank you, Leo," Tía Paloma said, squeezing Leo's shoulder.

"Use my bike," Caroline offered. "You should be

able to catch up with them if they're all walking."

Leo nodded, trying not to show her surprise. She was going to fix her mistake, and they believed in her.

It wouldn't just be a matter of following a trail, not if all the spirits had split up and the petals were scattered by the wind. And even if she had a guess about where each spirit might be heading, this wasn't like a game of hide-and-seek. She also had to bring them back, and they weren't going to come with her willingly.

How could she gather them all without making a scene and giving away their presence to the living people of the town? What if she couldn't get them back in time, and they disintegrated? What if this was more than she could handle?

Her doubts threatened to leak out of her mouth like pineapple jelly out of an empanada, but then her train of thought was interrupted by the blare of a phone. Caroline jumped, rushed to the wall next to the refrigerator, and answered with a high-pitched "Hello?"

The whole kitchen held its breath.

"Hello?" Caroline said again. "Is anybody there?" After a few long seconds, she pulled the phone from her ear, shrugged, and hung it back on its base. "Nobody," she said. She pressed a button on the phone. "Caller ID didn't recognize it. I thought it would be my dad checking in again, but I guess it was a wrong number?"

A mysterious call on a morning already full of spirits back from the dead was plenty spooky, but Leo wasn't thinking about that. She was thinking how she had called Caroline not too long ago, hoping to ask for help, and how that call hadn't gone the way she'd expected at all. She was back in the same position now, with too many imaginary timers ticking down to zero, and not enough people to deal with the problems. Maybe she should try a similar solution.

"Caroline," she said. "That reminds me. Can I borrow your cell phone? Um, in case I need to call when I'm out tracking the spirits." She was being sneaky again, but only a little. Caroline would understand later. She hoped.

"Sure." Caroline patted the pockets of her shorts. "I thought I had it. . . . I guess I left it in my room."

Leo followed Caroline through the living room, past the ladder to the attic in the middle of the hallway. They entered Caroline's room, and Leo stood in the doorway as her friend dug through her unmade bed and checked her bookshelves looking for her phone. Caroline's room had a new border of sunflowers and butterflies stenciled along the top of each wall, adding to the other hand-painted decorations. Mr. Campbell might need a new outlet for his creative energy.

On the bedside table Leo found the stolen candle—a fat yellow one, burned down now, with its tall sides curling up over the blackened wick deep in the center. Caroline had placed it next to the photo of her family, and in front of one of the flyers from this year's Rose Hill Day of the Dead Festival. Leo wondered if those could have contributed to the spell, but then, the bedside table also held a book about dragons, and the candle hadn't summoned any of those (that she knew of). She was glad Isabel and Tía Paloma were working on the reversal spell, but she did want to learn more about how it was done. There was so much she didn't know.

"How did it happen?" she asked. "And how did you know what was going on? I've never done a spell by accident, but it sounds scary."

"Well, I have been hanging out with you for the past three months," Caroline said. "So I guess I knew that what I was doing might cause *something* to happen. But at first I was confused. Mayor Rose was the first one to show up, just knocked on the door a few minutes after my dad left for work. And he can be really . . . intense. Then Mr. Nguyen, and

Mr. Pérez did the same thing. I almost thought the reyes magos had come early."

Leo laughed. The three spirits would make an odd trio of Christmas wise men. "I had Abuela with me," she said. "So I knew she was a spirit already. Well, I thought she was a ghost, but then we figured out she was, you know, touchable."

Caroline nodded. "That's good. I wasn't sure. Mayor Rose kept saying he had been 'sent'? I guess he was talking about the spell, but I thought he meant he was the plumber or something."

The explanation felt off to Leo. "You think the spell sent him to your house? Or drew him here? Why didn't Abuela feel it, then, or Mrs. Morales or Old Jack?"

"I don't know, but what else could have made three spirits knock on my door?" Caroline asked. "Maybe the other three were just the most stubborn ones."

Leo laughed and Caroline smiled. Her eyes darted around the room and her hands fiddled restlessly with her green beaded bracelet. "Where could my phone be?" she asked, biting her lip. "I had it when you called earlier, and I haven't gone anywhere."

"Did you bring it up to the attic?" Leo asked, checking between the piles of books Caroline kept on her desk because her bookshelf was too crowded. "When did you last have it?"

"This morning I was in the living room when you called, but then I came here"—Caroline turned to her bedside table—"to check that the candle was out. I thought that if your grandma had just appeared, the spell might still be going." She opened her closet and stared inside for a minute before shaking her head and closing the door. "But you said she showed up earlier, in the morning, right?"

"Yeah," Leo said. "At like seven o'clock." She knelt to check under the ruffled edge of Caroline's bed, but all she found were dust bunnies and marigold petals.

"Seven?" Caroline asked. "Are you sure? That means we're off again."

"Off what?" Leo had run out of searching ideas, so she smoothed out a spot on the comforter and settled onto the bed. This was why Isabel was always the one who found things in the Logroño house—she had more patience.

"Off on our count." Caroline came to stand by the bed, a crease forming between her eyebrows. "I have a theory that matches up, see? Because I lit the candle at midnight, and I thought I blew it out a little before seven—but I'm not positive. It could have been a few minutes after."

"What difference does it make if it was before or after seven?" Leo asked.

"Well, the ghosts—the spirits—didn't all show up at the same time," Caroline explained, sitting on the bed next to Leo. "Some came in the middle of the night, and some closer to dawn, and your grandma even later in the morning. They were all spaced out." Leo nodded, but Caroline must have known she wasn't following. She bounced on the bed as she continued, "I think one ghost came through each hour. So one at one a.m., one at two, and so on. If I blew the candle out at six fifty-something, six ghosts. But if I blew it out after seven . . ."

"Oh." Leo made a face. She hoped there wasn't one more spirit running free around town. "I guess we have to hope that you blew it out in time. Except . . . you know you're not supposed to *blow out* spell candles, right?"

Caroline shrugged. "No, I didn't know."

"You're never supposed to," Leo said, proud to share information memorized from her study packet. "It weakens the magic. Your spell was strong enough anyway, I guess. But it's a bad habit. Tía Paloma says brujas always cover their flames."

Leo knew she was being a little bit of a sabelotodo.

But she couldn't help it—she never got to be the one explaining a magic idea to someone else. And maybe she did let her voice get a little bit snooty, like Isabel sometimes did when she lectured.

But she didn't expect her words to make Caroline drop her head into her hands and burst into tears.

"Caroline?" Leo asked. "Are you . . . ?" Her friend's shoulders shook, so Leo decided not to finish that question. "It's okay," she said instead.

"No, it isn't." Caroline's voice was muffled but firm. "This is all wrong. I don't have any idea what I'm doing! I'm not a real bruja. This is all a disaster. I put people—ghost people—in danger. And if the whole town finds out about them? So many things could happen, and they're all bad! And why are you *smiling* at me?"

"I'm sorry!" Leo covered her mouth with her hands. "I'm sorry, I'm not smiling at anything you're saying. I'm just . . . smiling."

"It doesn't seem like anything to smile at." Caroline pouted.

"No," Leo agreed, "it's just that . . . well, those were all the same things I was thinking in November. I get it, and it's my turn to tell you that everything's going to be okay."

Caroline wiped her nose on the sleeve of her

flannel shirt. "Nothing you did was nearly as bad as this."

Leo hopped off the bed, because this required her to put her hands on her hips and stomp her foot for good measure. "Caroline Campbell, did I hear you correctly? Are you saying that your magic mishap is worse than mine? The whole entire school practically saw my love spell backfire! I shrank a boy! The police were out looking for Brent! Your spell hasn't made anyone call the police."

"Not yet," Caroline said, sticking out her bottom lip. "Not that we know of."

"Not at all," Leo insisted. "And nobody is going to. You're going to fix this, and then, well, then you'll figure out a way to learn more about your magic. And you'll practice and you'll get better—even if it's slow and boring sometimes—and we'll be the two best brujas in town. You'll see."

Caroline let out a long breath. "You think so?"

"Of course," Leo said. "Didn't you believe in me when I had to make an unraveling spell to unshrink Brent?"

"Um . . ." It was Caroline's turn to smile. "Maybe . . . ?"

Something buzzed on the other side of the room, making both girls jump and interrupting Leo's offended gasp. "My phone!" Caroline stood up and followed the buzzing underneath one of the open books on her desk. "That's so weird—how did it get . . ." She held the phone to her ear. "Hello? Hello-o-o?" She hung up, shrugging. "It's a blocked number," she said. "Like when you use star sixty-seven. My mom taught me that trick when I was tiny so we could prank call my aunts."

Leo wondered who would want to call Caroline with a blocked number.

"Here." Caroline held out the phone to Leo. "You should get going. Sorry it took me so long to find it."

"Thanks," Leo said. "That's weird, though. The mystery calls."

"Maybe it's just a bad connection," Caroline said, nodding like she was trying to convince herself. "We had a problem with that a couple years ago, when every time my grandma would try to call, it would cut out and we wouldn't hear anything. . . ."

Leo nodded too, even though she wasn't entirely convinced. With the way her and Caroline's day had been going, it seemed more likely to be a seventh spirit or a dragon or some other wild explanation.

"I should call her!" Caroline smacked her forehead. "My grandma. I can ask her if she knows anything about the curanderos in our family. I won't reveal your secrets, but I can at least talk."

"Great idea," Leo agreed. "We need all the help we can get." She had an urge to tell Caroline her plan, the real reason she wanted the cell phone. Caroline would understand. "In fact, I was thinking that—"

"Leo." Isabel knocked on the open door and peered into Caroline's room. "Are you ready to go?"

Leo clamped her mouth shut and wrapped her hand tightly around Caroline's cell phone. "I'm ready."

She followed Isabel back to the living room. Tía Paloma had spread multiple books on the floor around the coffee table and set an assortment of candles and small herb pouches on the tabletop. "Be careful," she intoned, barely looking up from her research.

"Wait." Abuela spoke behind her. "I'm coming with you."

Leo froze. "You are?"

"Of course," Abuela said. "It's as much my fault as yours that the others all got spooked and left, and you'll need someone who can knock Miguel Antonio upside the head if he gets too stubborn. Besides, this way you don't need a bike, because I can drive."

Leo nodded slowly. "Sure, I . . . I guess?"

"Oh, now, don't take me too seriously, Leonora."

Abuela linked arms with Leo and walked her out the front door onto the soggy front lawn. "There won't be any fighting, even with Miguel Antonio, I'm sure."

That wasn't what had Leo's stomach twisted in knots, but she shrugged and let Abuela lead her to the van, water from the ground seeping through the toes of her sneakers and making her socks sticky and cold. She had a plan for how to catch all the spirits, but it didn't seem like a plan she should share with Abuela.

"You know, Abuela," Leo said, fiddling with Caroline's cell phone in the pocket of her jeans. "Maybe we should split up. I could bike to the school and catch Mr. Nguyen. And you can drive to city hall and get started with Mayor Rose." Leo smiled and tried to shrug casually. "It would probably be faster."

Abuela stopped just in front of the van, turning to look at Leo with one hand on the passenger-side door. "You really think so, Leonora?"

Her dark eyes didn't blink, and Leo felt herself shrink from the gaze. But she squared her shoulders. This was important. Too much time had passed already. They needed to round up the spirits as quickly as possible.

"Sure," she squeaked, then cleared her throat

and calmed her voice to continue. "It's no problem. Caroline offered her bike already."

Abuela let out a long breath—did spirits need to breathe, Leo wondered, or did they just do it for dramatic effect?—and pulled open the passenger door. "Get in, Leonora."

Leo climbed into the van without another word of protest. While Abuela walked around and opened the driver door, Leo stared at the pattern her wet and muddy tennis shoes left on the already soggy floor of the van.

"I may be old. I may be dead. And I may be one solid breeze away from poofing into the star of some horror film," Abuela said, hunched forward to reach the steering wheel but pausing before turning on the engine. "But I'm still not gullible. So why don't you tell me the real reason you want to go off on your own?"

Leo winced. Where was Mrs. Morales when you needed her to distract Abuela with memories about high school? As sneaky and dishonest as she could sometimes be, Leo felt a bigger-than-average twinge of guilt at the thought of lying straight to Abuela's face.

"I wasn't trying to go off on my own," she said slowly. Abuela's eyebrows went up, and Leo lost all her defiance under the force of that disappointed expression. She pulled the cell phone out of her pocket and held it out like evidence, or like a plea. "I just want to find the spirits fast, and they're all in different places. So I was thinking, maybe . . ."

"Maybe?" Abuela tapped one finger against the steering wheel.

"I thought I could call some people," Leo finally admitted. "To help."

"Your friends," Abuela said. Leo nodded. "You wanted to get your non-brujo friends and get them involved, and you didn't want to tell your family you were doing it." She took the phone out of Leo's hands, turning it over thoughtfully.

Leo hung her head. "I just wanted to fix it," she said. "We need more hands to catch all the runaways." Runaways who only ran because she hadn't done her job.

Abuela turned the key, and the van engine grumbled. "So okay. What was your plan? Who were you going to call?"

"First I was going to knock on Brent Bayman's door, right there." She pointed to the house next to Caroline's. "And send him to the school after Mr. Nguyen. Then I'd go to city hall on the bike, and Tricia Morales can get her grandmother, who will hopefully be headed back to her house. And then you could use the car." Leo shrugged. "I don't know where the other spirits will be, but if you drive all around town, maybe . . ."

She stopped. Abuela was shaking her head.

"I know." Leo sighed. "We're not supposed to involve people outside the family in bruja business. We're supposed to be secretive. We're not even supposed to have nonmagical friends."

"That's what Isabel told you," Abuela stated flatly.

"And Marisol told me I should have friends, and that learning magic was the problem, and I shouldn't do it." Leo made a face at the dashboard. "It makes me wish . . ." She shook her head.

"Wish what?" Abuela asked.

Leo felt her throat squeeze inward. *Wish I had never found out about magic.* She couldn't say that, though. She didn't mean it. "We need to go," she said instead. "We're wasting time."

"Well, I'm trying to tell you," Abuela said. "Your plan is wrong. Leti Morales isn't going to her house. She's helping Miguel Antonio get to his sister."

"Oh." Leo frowned. "Okay. Is that around here?" Maybe all the spirits would stay near the center of town. Maybe she and Abuela would be just fine alone.

"It's out by Wide Oak Lane," Abuela answered, "close by Leti's house."

Leo groaned. That was still far from their current location. "What happens if we don't catch them?" she asked softly.

Abuela hesitated. "There might be a way to reverse the spell without the spirits being present, if your friend is very lucky and very clever," she said. "But if not—and I think it's unlikely—the spirits will wander until they tire out and disintegrate."

Leo frowned. "Then you shouldn't come with me. You should stay here so that you can get sent back the second they figure it out. You have to be careful."

Abuela smiled, releasing the steering wheel and turning to face Leo.

"Did you notice that each spirit that's come back has a purpose? Some unfinished business in the world of the living?"

Leo blinked. Old Jack's garden, Mr. Nguyen's piano, Mr. Pérez's apology to his sister . . . Abuela was right. "But you don't have one," she said. "Do you?"

Abuela smiled gently. "I showed up in your bedroom, Leo. Not in my house with Paloma. Not in my bakery. Because I wanted to talk."

"To me." Leo's face warmed. She was Abuela's

unfinished business. And that meant—her mouth dropped open in horror. It was her fault Abuela was in danger. "I'm . . . I'm sorry."

Abuela waved away her apology with a flap of one hand. "Leo, your sisters don't know everything."

"I know." Leo shrugged.

"They're still young, and still figuring out their places in life," Abuela continued. "And their places in the family, in the community. Same as you. And what's best for them—when it comes to secrets, and family, and friends—might not always be what's best for you."

"Really?" A tight knot of worry in Leo's chest started to loosen.

Abuela smiled softly. "It wasn't always a secret, our magic. Back when this town first sprang up, people knew. It's right there in the name of the bakery: Amor y Azucar. First and foremost, our magic is about love. Love for our family and our friends, for our customers and our town. Magic should strengthen relationships, not sever them."

The words swept over Leo like a wave, like music, flooding her emotions even quicker than Isabel's influence. "I knew it," she whispered fiercely. Then the wave crashed. "I should have known it." She frowned. "I'm sorry, Abuela. I should have known it and then you wouldn't have been pulled through and you wouldn't be in danger of going poof and—"

"Leonora," Abuela said. "Cálmate."

The soft Spanish word sparked a memory: a party in the backyard of the Logroño house, Leo crying into the front of her purple-and-white Easter dress because Marisol had smashed cascarones on her head and the broken eggshell and confetti pieces dug into her scalp and tangled in her hair. Daddy was breaking up a fight between his two sisters, and Mamá was keeping the twins from picking on their cousin J.P., so it was Abuela's hands that had scooped Leo into the air, patted her back, and worked the debris out of her ponytail. It was Abuela's voice that had whispered, "Cálmate, Leonora, mijita linda."

Leo didn't know until that moment that she had any memories of Abuela alive, and she squeezed her eyes shut to concentrate on locking this one into her brain where she would never lose it again.

"I didn't come here just for you," Abuela said. "I wanted to talk to you first, because you needed help immediately, to fix things with Caroline. But that wasn't the only reason." Abuela sighed, her eyes flicking to the green-glowing clock on the van's dashboard—10:41. "I'm afraid now that we're running out of time, so I may need to trust you with delivering the message to Isabel and Marisol. I don't want you all to grow up thinking that you have to choose between being a bruja and having good friends, isolating yourselves because of something that should be connecting you. If I had gotten that same advice, Leti and I would never have been best friends!"

Understanding sparked like Christmas lights in Leo's mind. "Abuela, are you saying . . . ?"

"I'm saying you're right; we won't be able to do this alone." Abuela put the cell phone back in Leo's hands. "Call your friends."

CHAPTER 13

CALLING ALL SPIRIT HUNTERS

"The spirits drop these orange petals," Leo explained to Brent Bayman. "So you can follow any trails you see. Mr. Nguyen should be easy to spot, since the school will be mostly empty. Are you sure you can do this?"

"Oh, I can find him," Brent said, showing off shiny braces in a wide smile and squeezing the brakes of the bicycle he perched on with one foot on the ground. "I'm just worried about what happens once I do. Are you sure I shouldn't have some kind of, I don't know, equipment?"

"This isn't *Ghostbusters*," Leo said. "They're just

regular people." Brent raised his eyebrows, and Leo sighed. "Who are dead and are actually spirits pulled through the veil, yes, okay. But my point is you just need to talk to him and explain that he needs to come back to Caroline's or else he might disappear forever. Use your words."

"Use your words," Brent grumbled. "Sure, everyone else gets magic and spells, and I get 'use your words.'" He stuck out his tongue and smiled, though, so Leo knew he wasn't really mad.

Brent had found out about Leo's magic the hard way, when Leo accidentally made him fall in love with the whole school and then shrank him to the size of a gingerbread man, which could be why he had taken the news of Caroline's new powers in stride, staying totally calm except for one long loud whistle of surprise. He had greeted Abuela cheerfully, having met her last November when he was two inches tall and she was a regular ghost. And best of all, he had shown no hesitation when Leo asked for his help tracking down a piano-obsessed spirit—though he had made Leo promise him free bakery goodies if he helped her out.

In fact, the only part of this whole situation he found unreasonable was his lack of proper weaponry. It made Leo want to laugh—and maybe also cry—that her friend trusted her even after all the trouble her magic had caused him.

"So I'll find him, and I'll bring him back here, and I'll meet up with you and your spirits and everyone, and you will pay me back with free cake." Brent nodded, clipped his green-and-blue helmet under his chin, and lifted his foot to coast down the driveway. "Sounds good. Last one back has the sulfuric odor but none of the compostable nutrients of a rotten egg!"

Leo nodded and waved, rolling her eyes a little. Abuela honked from the van, and Leo hopped into the passenger seat, buckling her seat belt as Abuela followed Brent to the end of the block. She pulled out the phone once more.

"Go ahead, Leonora," Abuela said.

Leo nodded but gulped. Brent, even though he was a tough negotiator, was the easy one. Calling Tricia was more complicated. Just a few hours ago, Leo had lied to her friend's face. How angry would Tricia be when Leo told her the truth? But there was no other way. She found Tricia's name in Caroline's contacts, gritted her teeth, and tapped the call button. She needed the help, and if her friend hated her after this was over, then she would be getting what she deserved.

The phone rang. And rang. Leo squeezed her eyes shut.

"Caroline? What's up?"

Leo had totally forgotten which phone she was calling from.

"Hi, Tricia," she said. "It's actually Leo. I'm using Caroline's phone."

"Oh!" Tricia said. "Did you two make up? I knew you would. Mai's here now, and we . . ." Mai's voice shouted something muffled. "Yes, you two should come over! We can do a mini snack-club meeting—I have brownie mix, I think."

"Wait," Leo said. "Um, I have something sort of . . . huge to tell you. And I need to ask a big favor."

"Are you okay?" Tricia asked. "Is everything okay with your family?"

"Yes, yes, we're all fine. We're just . . ." Leo glanced at Abuela, who nodded. "This is so weird," Leo whispered to her grandmother before speaking into the phone in one giant rush. "My family and I are actually brujas? And there are a bunch of spirits on the loose because of a spell that went wrong and . . . well, Caroline's involved too, but we're not exactly sure how that works, but I sort of need help catching them? And one of them is your grandma, so I probably should have told you that when I saw you this morning. But I didn't. Sorry. She left your dad a note, but I stole it. Sorry again. Anyway, you don't have to help, but it's really important that we find them and we need more people, and oh, and do you mind telling Mai? That way you can both work together. It's okay, she can know about our secret too, I trust her."

Tricia was silent. Leo heard rustling and crackling noises and wondered if Tricia was about to hang up on her. The phone beeped, and a slightly muffled voice asked, "Hello?"

"Mai?"

"You're on speaker," Tricia said. "Because I definitely don't want to try to explain this conversation. So just start over, please? And tell us what you need us to do."

As Abuela turned onto Main Street, Leo took a breath and told her friends everything, starting with discovering her family's secret magic back in November.

Abuela pulled into the city hall parking lot as Leo gave Tricia and Mai the directions to Mr. Pérez's sister's house, as best Abuela could remember them. She hung up the phone, nervous sweat drying as she let out a long breath. She'd told someone about magic, on purpose. Nobody—not Mamá, or Tía Paloma, or Isabel or Marisol—would approve of that. And then she had sent three nonmagical friends off to hunt spirits, armed only with cell phones and vague descriptions.

What the heck was she thinking?

She didn't have time for second thoughts, though, because Abuela cut the engine and unbuckled her seat belt. "So. Mayor Rose. What's the plan here?" she asked Leo. "Do you want me to go in with you?"

Leo weighed the risk of someone recognizing Abuela against how much she didn't want to walk into the very official-looking building on her own. "No, that's okay,' she said with a grimace. "You can stay here."

Abuela smirked. "I always wanted to be a getaway driver. Unfinished business number two, checked off the list."

Leo only half laughed as she left the van and jogged up the wheelchair ramp of the city hall. It was smaller than the lower school and the movie theater, but it had a tall clock tower and walls made of shiny white stone, and the doors were made of metal with flowers and vines molded into their surfaces. Leo tugged them open and stepped onto the shiny white tile floor, straight into the sights of one of the old church ladies Mamá knew, someone who gossiped over doughnuts with the other church ladies and who would definitely recognize Abuela or anyone else from town who had died in the past thirty or so years.

Good thing Mayor Rose was a lot older than that, or he'd have been recognized the second he walked through the doors.

"Hello," the woman said. "Leo Logroño? What are you doing here?"

Leo smiled a big desperate smile as her brain spiraled in a frenzy, whipping her thoughts into a froth. She couldn't use the same lie she had at the hardware store; the church lady wouldn't fall for a mysterious great-uncle that she'd never met or heard of without getting suspicious. She searched the room and caught sight of a few orange petals bunched against the wall under a bulletin board of town information. The cork backing was crumbling, and two red balloons trailed limply on the ground, mostly deflated but still stapled to the top of the board. The pile of ragged petals made the whole thing look even more abandoned, but they meant Mayor Rose had been here. She just needed to know what he had done and where he was now.

"Leo?" the church lady asked. "Is everything all right?"

"I . . ." Leo gulped. "I had a question about the mayor election." She paused, hoping the church lady would mention another man who had been in here asking about the election, but instead the woman blinked at Leo through her narrow glasses.

"The *mayoral* election?" she asked. "Why do you want to know about that?"

Leo blinked back. "Um, no reason," she said.

This was apparently the wrong answer. Church Lady straightened her glasses, threw back her shoulders, and fixed Leo with a disapproving glare that made her look a lot like Abuela. "Miss Leo, I hope I don't have to tell your mamá that you were involved in the recent incident of *vandalism*," she said harshly.

"Vandalism?" Leo squeaked. "No, I didn't do that. I don't even know what that is!"

Church Lady produced several medium-sized posters from behind her desk and held them out for Leo to inspect. "Vandalism is a criminal act of defacing property . . . like these mayoral campaign signs that were defaced, just minutes before you show up with questions about the election."

Leo looked at the posters, which showed the smiling but grainy faces of two women who both shared Mayor Rose's wide smile. Unfortunately, those smiles had almost been covered by big permanent-marker block letters written on top of the posters. *Rose Hill Needs Real Leaders* read the first sign, and the second sign added *The Past Is the Way to the Future.* Whoever had written the messages—and Leo had a pretty good idea of who that was—had also drawn thick frowning eyebrows on one candidate and greedy dollar signs over the second one's eyes.

"Oh no," Leo said. "Where did this happen?"

"Just down the road," Church Lady answered. "They were brought to my attention by a concerned citizen. Are you telling me this wasn't your doing?"

"No!" Leo said. "I wouldn't do that."

Church Lady hummed skeptically. "And you don't know anything about it?"

Leo hesitated for a second too long before she answered, "Uh, no?"

"I knew it!" Church Lady threw the posters to the ground with surprising force for such a small woman. "You're an accomplice, probably going around with some hooligan friends, getting into trouble. Are you here to distract me so your friends can cause more property damage?"

"No!" Leo cringed away from the yelling. "I'm not here with any hooligans. I was just thinking that I did see some teenagers running around outside. Maybe they were the vandalismers." Leo mentally apologized to teenagers everywhere, who probably had enough problems without getting blamed for things that were actually the fault of hundred-year-old ghosts.

Church Lady squinted at Leo. "Are you sure?" She asked. "Were they students at Rose Hill High? I should report this to the proper authorities." She picked up the bulky old telephone on the desk.

"Wait!" Leo held up her hand. "Reporting" sounded like it could get people into trouble, and what if the proper authorities started searching and found Mayor Rose? She couldn't let that happen. "Um, I don't know if they were students. But I don't think they meant any harm. They were probably just . . ." What was the word Mamá used when Marisol messed up? "Acting out. And school is out right now anyway. Plus, I don't think it will happen again. Teenagers get bored easily. It's probably better if you don't make a big deal out of it."

Church Lady tapped her nails against the desk, and Leo put on her widest and most convincing smile.

"Well, you might be right," she finally sad. "No sense in letting them know they've riled me up. And I guess, in their own way, the vandals are engaging in the democratic process. I just wish they'd find a more constructive way to make their voices heard." She rolled her eyes and shook her head.

Leo nodded. "That's actually what I wanted to ask about," she said. "I came here to learn more about the election for mayor. Like, when is it? Who are we voting for? Is it too late to enter the running? Is it true that there are some towns that have cats for mayors? I saw that on the internet."

Church Lady's very annoyed glare relaxed into a slightly annoyed smile. "Well, regardless of what the internet might tell you, young lady, our elections are a very serious matter, and vital to the health and security of our town. You wouldn't want a cat deciding when to repave the roads or where your school band could hold a fund-raiser, would you?"

Leo shook her head.

"I should think not." Church Lady tutted and shuffled through the box of papers at the front of her desk. "Now, if you want to get involved and learn more about the candidates, you should read these statements from each of them. Talk about the issues with your parents, and oh—" She dug deeper in her desk and produced a brightly colored pamphlet. "We have a youth summer program you can apply for. We are planning a field trip to the state capital in Austin, if we get enough interest. And don't worry so much about the deadline on there; there are plenty of spots." She glanced sadly down at the pamphlet before smiling as she held it out to Leo.

"Um, thanks." Leo took the stack of papers.

"As for your other questions, the election is right around the corner." Church Lady smiled and added another flyer to Leo's pile. "So make sure to remind your family to vote!"

Leo nodded. The bright orange flyer in her hands listed the date of the election, only a few weeks away, along with all the official candidates for all the different positions. There was no way Mayor Rose could enter this late.

"Does that answer all your questions, dear?" Church Lady asked.

"I think so." Leo sighed. She turned and speed-walked away from Church Lady, pausing in front of the bulletin board on her way out to notice that several flyers had also been vandalized with a Sharpie and now read *Write in Rose for Mayor!*

Leo snatched the flyers and waved at the church lady, who reminded Leo to say hi to Mamá. Leo skipped the ramp and hopped down the front steps three at a time.

"He was here, but he isn't anymore," she told Abuela. She shoved Church Lady's pamphlets and the ruined flyers onto the dashboard. "It's too late to run for office. He probably figured that out, and then he must have left."

"Okay," Abuela said. "But then where did he go?"

Leo held up her hands. "How should I know?" The snap in her voice came from fear, not anger, but she felt guilty when she saw Abuela frown at her. "I mean, I'm not sure," she corrected herself. "I don't have any ideas of where to look."

Caroline's phone chirped in her pocket, and she checked the screen before answering. "Tricia? Did you find them?"

"Sorry, Leo," Tricia said. "The lady who lives in the purple house said that Mr. Pérez's sister moved three years ago. And she said nobody else had knocked all day, and we didn't see any marigold petals anywhere. Wherever he is, he didn't come to the house."

"Okay." Leo bit her lip. "Did she say where she moved to? Maybe we can find her new address?"

"Nope, she moved to Wisconsin."

Leo's stomach fell like the city hall balloons with no helium left to keep them upright.

"What should we do?" Tricia asked.

Leo could only think of one answer. "Just forget it," she whispered. "We aren't finding them in the places we expected, and I don't have a plan B. We should all probably go back . . ." *Home,* she wanted to finish the sentence, but she choked on the word.

"To Caroline's house. Great. We'll meet you there in twenty minutes." Tricia hung up the phone before Leo could unstick her throat.

"What happened?" Abuela asked. "Your friends didn't find Leti either?"

Leo shook her head. "Mr. Pérez can't talk to his sister either, unless he's going to fly to Wisconsin. So now we go back, I guess, and hope that Caroline or Isabel found something to save the day." Leo clutched Caroline's cell phone tightly, her stomach churning with frustration. "There wasn't even any point in telling my friends our secret, I guess." She looked up at Abuela, whose eyes looked soft and sorry for Leo. It made her feel even worse, because she was supposed to be saving Abuela from disintegration. This wasn't about Leo. "Can you just drive us back?"

"Hmm." Abuela pulled the van out of its parking spot, screeching the tires as she drove too fast in reverse. "Sorry, but no. That is not what we're going to do."

"What do you mean?"

"Leonora," Abuela said as she turned onto Main

Street, "I may not have much time left to teach you things, so I need you to listen to me. We are brujas cocineras. Our family solves problems. We do not give up. So you are going to call your friends back and tell them to meet us at the bakery, and we are going to figure this out. Okay?"

Leo turned away from Abuela's determined grin and stared out the window. She couldn't imagine how this problem could be solved, but she believed her grandmother. "Okay, I guess."

Abuela nodded firmly, showering petals down the front of her sweater. She rolled through a stop sign, her laugh ringing loud as she sped down the street. When Leo turned to look at her grandmother's face, the thin lines at the corners of her eyes had shrunk and nearly disappeared.

"Hurry," Leo said, more to herself than her fast-driving abuela. "We're running out of time."

CHAPTER 14

OJOS DE BUEY

She checked in with Caroline before calling Tricia back.

"I called my grandmother in Costa Rica," Caroline said. "She didn't want to talk about it so much, but my prima got on and told me about my great-uncle, who was the last brujo in our family."

Since her family magic was all possessed by generations of women, Leo had almost forgotten that men could be brujos too. "So what did you learn about him?"

"It's so cool, Leo! She told me all the history that I didn't know anything about! My family were curanderos at first, helping their neighbors with their problems and healing their illnesses. And then when people had gotten so used to coming to my family for help . . . they started coming even after they died. And as they did, my ancestors developed some magical ability, so they could help put spirits to rest. That's been our family gift for generations now. My great-uncle's talent was for finding crossroads that were haunted by restless spirits. They wouldn't be walking around like our spirits, totally pulled into the living world, but sometimes they would be stuck trying to cross, or they would be fighting to get themselves back on this side. He would help dispel them."

"Okay." Leo wasn't sure she liked how close "dispel" was to "disintegrate," but if Caroline didn't sound worried, then she wasn't going to bring it up. "So you kind of did the opposite of that with your accidental spell."

"Your aunt thinks it's good news," Caroline explained, "because if I can bring them here, that may mean that I can send them back."

"Yeah, that makes sense." Leo nodded. "Oh! And Caroline, do you already know about everyone's unfinished business? Abuela told me that all the spirits have some, so that makes perfect sense."

"Yeah, I noticed that when they first started showing up," Caroline said excitedly. Leo wasn't surprised that her clever friend had figured out the pattern before she had. "It fits my family magic pattern, right? If we're supposed to help ghosts find peace. And it explains why the spell didn't work how I was hoping, and didn't bring back—I mean, why these particular spirits were pulled through to our world."

"Right," Leo said. "Of course."

"But it's weird that there are so many," Caroline said. "My prima said in Costa Rica there might be one restless spirit every five years or something. That's why my grandma never bothered to learn the spells from her uncle. I know my spell helped them cross, but why are there so many restless spirits in Rose Hill?"

"I don't know," Leo said. "But now I want to find out."

"Anyway, how's it going on your end?"

"Oh, um, fine, I think." Leo didn't want to lie to Caroline, so she changed the subject. "Will you be ready to unravel the spell when we get them back to you?"

"I think we will!" Caroline said. "Except Isabel says it's not strictly unraveling, because we were afraid that just undoing the effects of the spell would hurt the spirits without sending them to the right side of the veil. So she and your aunt found the basic outline for a portal spell—something to open a gate between different worlds. Your aunt isn't very happy about it, because it's not a very safe spell or something, but we're going to modify that with some unraveling elements and do our best to make sure it gets our spirits back safely. We should be ready for a test"—Leo could hear Isabel's voice in the background—"in about an hour."

"Perfect," Leo said, hoping Caroline couldn't hear the concern in her voice. She didn't know how they could round up the spirits in an hour, given the fact that they'd made zero progress. "I'll let you get back to it. See you soon."

"Sounded like an interesting conversation," Abuela prompted after Leo sat for a minute too long staring at the phone in her lap without saying anything.

"Sorry, yes, it was." Leo shook her head. "It's good news, mostly. I'm just worried that Caroline will be ready before we've found anyone. But she found out about her family magic, and she has an idea about how to send you home!"

She checked the van's clock while she filled Abuela

in on the details of her conversation. It was past eleven, so the bakery would be hitting its busiest hour. Abuela popped on a pair of Mamá's sunglasses as she navigated the parking lot to reach a free spot close to the back door. Leo updated Tricia and left a message for Brent, who didn't answer his phone. "Meet us at the bakery. Change of plans. Hurry!"

"I have a theory," Abuela said. "To answer your friend's question." She was staring out the window at the line of people entering and exiting the bakery.

"You do?" Leo asked. "Wait, which question?"

"Why so many spirits from Rose Hill were so quick to cross the veil."

"Why?" Leo asked.

"I think it has to do with the bakery. With our family taking root here and weaving our magic into the community."

"Wait, so it's our fault there are so many unhappy spirits?" Leo asked, frowning.

"Not unhappy," Abuela said. "Just . . . active. Many people here in town actually eat magic for breakfast. That's got to rub off on you after a while."

"Oh." Leo looked out the window and imagined each person leaving the bakery with a paper bag full of magic. "That's cool."

"I think so." Abuela smiled. "That's why it's

important for you girls to help your mamá and learn about the bakery. I can't imagine what the town would be without it."

Abuela let her bun out—the white streaks had almost entirely disappeared from her shiny smooth curtain of hair—and they ducked into the kitchen like fugitive spies.

"What are you doing here?" Alma yelped when Leo opened the back door and almost collided with the hot tray her sister carried. "Leo's back!" she called over her shoulder. "And . . . is this another spirit?"

Abuela laughed loud, pulled her hair back over her shoulder, and slid the glasses up to the top of her head. Alma yelped again.

"Abuela?" Belén appeared at her twin's shoulder. "Is that you? You look like a movie star!"

"I feel tired," Abuela grumbled over her smile. "Are you girls keeping busy?"

"Too busy," Belén complained. "Mamá is either going to die of happiness or exhaustion with how many customers we've had today."

"Mom?" Mamá said. She had two hands full of mixing bowls and a streak of flour across her cheek. "What are you doing back here?"

"Leo and I need to take over the office for a little

while," Abuela said, her hands reaching out to rub Mamá's shoulders. "You're okay out here, Maria Elena?"

Mamá closed her eyes and rolled her shoulders into Abuela's touch. "Of course," she said. She shoved aside a few dirty spoons to make room for her bowls on the counter and turned to give Abuela a proper hug. "It's good to see you," she said softly. "To *really* see you."

"Oh, hush, no it isn't." Abuela patted Mamá's back and laughed. "I don't belong here, and you have plenty to do without me showing up and causing a fuss. Keep it up, mija. You're doing good. I'll be back where I belong before you know it."

Mamá held on tight for another long breath, then released Abuela and wiped the now-wet flour off her cheek. "Okay. Good."

"You just worry about keeping my bakery running," Abuela said.

"Alma, Belén, the frosting?" Mamá ordered. The twins reluctantly returned to their stations, adding the finishing touches to another batch of rosca de reyes. Leo followed Abuela to the office and shut the door behind them.

"All right, Leonora." Abuela stooped to pull a book off the office shelf. "Your tía and sister have the important job of testing out new magics to deal with this very unusual problem. But in times of crisis, I like to go with something tried and trusted." She let the heavy book slam onto Daddy's desk, and Leo recognized the red leather cover of the family recipe book. A smile crept into the corners of her mouth.

"You think there's a spell in there that can help?"

Abuela's loud, short laugh was becoming familiar, settling into Leo's brain like Señor Gato kneading the couch cushions into shape and curling up in them.

"I sure hope so, Leonora. If not, I'm in deep caca."

Ojo de Buey Buscador: estos pasteles te ayudarán a ver claro, e iluminarán el camino para encontrar cosas perdidas.

The spell for finding lost things was as simple as lifting the couch cushions and finding your keys, but as tedious as searching every other room of the house before remembering to check the cushions. Mamá had the pastry dough ready-made, but Leo had to make the batter for the inner muffin—the mantecada—from scratch, sifting the flour three times, while adding a layer of magic by thinking of things so light and fluffy that they were nearly transparent. She added the sugar, butter, and other ingredients quickly, stirring "with urgency" so the spell would understand. She sniffed the orange essence before Abuela added it to the mixture, "while holding the lost object or objects in your mind." And lastly, as she poured the batter into each circle of pastry dough, she added one eyelash to the top of each, and then blew it away. They made six ojos de buey, and Alma and Belén each contributed a few eyelashes so that Leo wouldn't have to pull so many of her own.

The ojos de buey were in the oven when Tricia and Mai knocked on the back door. Leo showed them where to lock their bikes and ushered them into the office, making sure to stay between them and the ovens so nobody got burned.

"It looks so serious back here," Mai whispered, dark eyes glued to the stainless steel of the oversized appliances. "It doesn't look how I imagined it."

She seemed much happier with the look of the recipe book, which was old and handwritten and appropriately witchy. She also kept Daddy's rolling chair between herself and Abuela. "That's a ghost?" she whispered to Tricia.

Abuela gave a wolflike smile and waved her arms

until petals fluttered to the floor.

"Oo-oo-ooh," she moaned, and then laughed when Mai jumped and screamed. "Sorry, don't pay any attention to me. I'm a jerk, but I think I'm funny. I'm glad to meet you, and I'm grateful for your help."

Mai nodded, short black pigtails wobbling, but she didn't come out from behind the chair.

"You don't look like an abuela," Tricia pointed out, eyeing Abuela suspiciously and looking ready to join Mai in the corner.

"She's aging in reverse," Leo explained. "We have to find all the spirits and send them back quickly, before they stop existing altogether."

Mai's eyes were wide. "If she ages backward and stops existing, does that mean your mom and you were never born?"

Leo hid her giggle behind her hand, but Abuela did not. "No," she explained while Mai turned red. "It's just the spirits who are in danger of becoming real ghosts, the restless haunting kind. It doesn't erase the things I did while I was alive."

"Don't worry." Tricia elbowed Mai sympathetically. "I don't have any idea what's happening either. Welcome to Leo's world."

"I'm sorry," Leo said. "I know this is a lot to take in. And I'm sorry for not telling you the truth sooner.

But everything is happening so fast, and I . . . I can't do this by myself. I need my snack club."

Mai and Tricia exchanged a glance, then nodded. "We don't mind helping," Mai said. "I mean, this is really weird, but exciting."

"I always wanted to be a Ghostbuster," Tricia added.

"And I'll try to explain better," Leo promised. "We have about five minutes before the ojos de buey are ready—there's a spell on them that will help us find out where the spirits have gone."

She was halfway through explaining the plan when Alma opened the office door.

"Leo, your friend is at the front counter acting extremely suspicious and freaking out customers. Will you please come get him?"

"What?" Leo, Tricia, and Mai scrambled to follow Alma. The four girls burst through the swinging blue doors to the sight of Brent Bayman arguing with Daddy through a mouthful of empanada.

"But we had a deal," he said indignantly. "Ask Leo! I've been helping her out, and I earned these, fair and square!"

"I'm sorry, Brent, but you can't help yourself to free food, no matter what Leo said." Daddy sounded tired, his friendly customer voice stretched tight, like it was ready to break. "And you, sir," he called to an old man behind Brent, "I need you to pay for that. I hope you're not going to tell me you've made a deal with my daughter as well."

Leo and Mai gasped in unison as the gray-haired customer turned around, petals stirring beneath his feet and a half-eaten concha hanging from his mouth. His hair was thicker and the skin around his eyes was smooth, but there was no mistaking the shiny silver glasses or the face that had taught all of them to breathe from their diaphragm.

Brent had found Mr. Nguyen.

"Believe me," the spirit said, "I didn't willingly enter into any deals with these children. In fact—"

"Daddy!" Leo rushed to the front of the counter and tugged his sleeve. "Um, can I talk to you?"

"Leonora." Daddy sounded cheerful, but his arched eyebrows told a different story. "I hear you've been making some promises to your friends."

"Yes." Leo twisted her hands around each other. The bakery was still full of customers, and even if they weren't all exactly staring straight at her, it felt like they were. "Um, it was a special situation?"

"The ends justify the means, is that it?" Mr. Nguyen asked bitterly. Leo didn't know how Brent had gotten him here at all if he was so grumpy about it, but she couldn't ask right in front of everyone.

"Leo, you can't be giving out free buffet passes to your friends. If you—" Daddy stopped when he finally noticed Leo's eyebrows hopping up and down. "Oh," he said. "A *special* circumstance." He sighed. "Why don't you both go talk to your mother about this?" He raised his voice for the customers to hear better. "She'll explain why we can't be giving out our wares for free." He winked an apology at Brent, shook his head at Leo, and gave them both a push toward the kitchen. "And you, sir—"

"Oh, he's coming with us," Leo said quickly. "He's the . . . repair . . . person . . ." She lost steam with her lie, but luckily Daddy didn't need any more hints.

"Of course. Glad you were able to make it. We really did need that specialty oven part. Leo will show you back to the kitchen." He made a face at Leo, who shrugged. "Now, who's waiting to check out?" He returned to the cash register while Leo and her friends dragged a grumbling Mr. Nguyen back to the kitchen.

"What were you thinking?" Alma whisper-hissed at Leo as soon as they were safe.

"What were *you* thinking?" Leo turned to Brent, who was looking way too pleased with himself and his empanada.

"Why didn't you tell us that Mr. Nguyen was one of the people who came back?" Mai asked Leo in a whisper, looking at the spirit with a less nervous smile. Mr. Nguyen's grouchy face softened a bit when he saw her, and he greeted her with a pat on the head that she didn't cringe away from.

"You said to come to the bakery." Brent shrugged. "It took us a little longer since we didn't both fit on my bike, and I got hungry. You did say I could have free samples for life."

Leo breathed in through her nose and counted to ten like Isabel always told Marisol to do. She tried to remember that she needed her friends' help and that she was grateful. "Thank you," she said between clenched teeth. "For finding him. Good job. Just so you know, there is a back door you can use for sensitive things like delivering wayward spirits."

"Or blackmailing them," Mr. Nguyen muttered.

Brent shrugged again. "Okay, okay, I get it. Where are the rest of the flower ghosts?"

"Uh . . ." Leo kicked a crack in the orange-tiled floor. "We didn't exactly find anyone else."

Brent's eyebrows shot up. "Really? Yes! I'm the best Ghostbuster!" He raised his fists in triumph.

"Brent!" Leo smacked his arm while Tricia rolled her eyes. "That's bad news. They're in danger, and we need to find them."

Brent grimaced and opened his mouth, probably to apologize, but Mamá shouted them out of her path as she came by with a hot tray. Leo gathered her friends back into the office, where they would be slightly crowded but not in the way.

"What are you doing back?" Mai was asking Mr. Nguyen. "There aren't problems in your family too, are there?"

"No, no, nothing to worry about, cháu," Mr. Nguyen assured her. "It was an entirely professional issue that brought me to the school. My piano"—he frowned at Brent as he said it—"was in terrible condition."

"Weird," Brent said. "Mr. Nguyen has a family?"

Leo rolled her eyes along with Tricia and Mai, even though she did think it was a little bit weird for teachers to have lives and families outside of school. But she knew not to say it.

"Yeah, he's my uncle," Mai said. "Not my real uncle, but I call him my uncle. He knows my parents."

"Say hello to them for me," Mr. Nguyen said.

Mai raised her eyebrows and shook her head. "Um, you're a ghost."

Mr. Nguyen nodded slowly. "Good point. On second thought, maybe it's best if you don't."

"Yeah, don't get any ideas." Brent wagged a

warning finger at Mr. Nguyen. "Everything I said still applies if anyone besides the people in this room finds out you're really a ghost."

Mr. Nguyen threw up his hands. "I agreed already, Mr. Bayman. Honestly, this is why I never taught middle school."

"Agreed to what?" Leo said. Brent looked awfully guilty. "What did you tell him?"

"Well, I had to convince him to come with me somehow," Brent said. "He didn't want to leave the piano to follow some random kid, and *someone* didn't give me any magic shrink rays to use on him."

"I don't have magic shrink—" Leo started, but Mr. Nguyen interrupted her.

"He threatened to destroy my piano after I left this world."

"What?" Tricia gasped.

"Brent!" Leo scolded.

"Dang." Mai nodded at Brent. "Good thinking." Mr. Nguyen gave her his disappointed teacher face.

"Thank you." Brent pointed at Mai. "I didn't exactly see anyone else capture their spirits. Besides, I also promised I'd check in on the piano every month or so if he cooperated."

Leo wanted to tell him that threats were not what she had meant by "using your words," but Belén knocked on the office door and poked her head in. "Leo, your timer's done."

"I'll grab them," Abuela said from where she had been leaning against one corner of Mamá's desk, looking like she might like to escape herself. She jumped to unload the spelled pan dulce, and Leo made sure all her friends kept a safe distance from the oven and burning tray as they followed her into the kitchen.

"They look . . . normal," Tricia said, eyeing the ojos de buey as they cooled.

"I mean, they look kind of weird," Mai argued. "Is it a pie filled with cake?"

Leo shrugged. "Kind of? Or like a muffin with crust. You can't see the spell, but once you take a bite, you'll be able to tell."

"Mysterious," Mai said, picking up one of the hot pastries off the cooling rack and then dropping it.

"Yep," Leo said. She didn't mention that the spell, and how it would work, was still a mystery to her as well.

They stared impatiently at the rack of baked goods. The smell of the spongy muffins filled Leo's nose, accompanied by a whiff of spicy magic. "All right, I'm going in," Brent said, picking up one of the circular ojos with the tips of his fingers. "We just have to take a bite?"

Leo glanced at Abuela, who nodded. Brent bit into the ojo de buey, cracking the harder outer layer, and ripped off a chunk of the squishy inside. Mai followed, then Leo and Tricia. After some consideration, Abuela and Mr. Nguyen decided to split one, even though they weren't sure the spell would work on spirits.

"Did it work?" Brent asked with his mouth stuffed full. "Do ooo see anyfing?"

Leo nibbled the still-hot edge of her ojo de buey. "I don't—oh."

She gasped as glowing lines started to streak in front of her eyes like lightning. Her vision filled with them until she had to cover her face with her hands, but she could still see the storm of shifting lights, stronger than afterimages. Just when she thought her head might burst, the storm stopped. She slowly uncovered her face and opened her eyes.

A dim crisscross of golden-orange lines stayed visible, their edges shifting when she stared too hard. One short thick one looped lazily around the kitchen, while others stretched straight through walls to cut the room into sections.

"Are these . . . ?"

"Ha ha, look." Brent prodded Mr. Nguyen, who

stepped away with a grunt of protest. When he moved, he left a thick line of light behind him, which shed pieces of itself to become the trail of marigold petals.

"Whoa," Tricia whispered. "Wild."

"Did your spell make these?" Mai reached out to touch the golden light, but her hand passed through it like the beam of a projector.

Leo shrugged, resisting the urge to touch the nearest light to see if it felt like anything.

"Actually, the spell only affects your eyes," Abuela said. "The energy trails, the magic we leave behind, were always here. Now we can all see them, which will make it easier to find our friends." She clapped her hands and brushed crumbs off her sweater. "So now that we can track them, let's get started. Leo? What's the plan?"

CHAPTER 15

ON THE HUNT

The plan was to split up. Tricia and Mai, who would be walking, took one of the lights that seemed the most strong and steady, as they assumed that meant that their spirit was close by. Leo partnered with Brent, whose bike had pegs on the wheels for a second person to stand on, and they chose the next brightest thread. Abuela and Mr. Nguyen would take the van to track the thinnest stretched path.

"You're sure you'll behave?" Leo asked. "Both of you? And come right back here when you find your spirit?"

"Cross my heart and hope to . . . well, you know

what I mean," Abuela teased.

"I'm still being coerced with the threat of piano violence," Mr. Nguyen said woefully.

"That's right." Brent nodded. "I know where the science teachers keep all the weird chemicals. I bet it wouldn't do your piano any favors if I dumped some of them inside."

"Middle schoolers," Mr. Nguyen muttered sadly, shaking his head as he followed Abuela to the parking lot.

"Okay." Leo looked at her friends. "We find the spirits. We use our charm and our logic—"

"—or threats if necessary," Mai added.

"But hopefully not," Leo continued, "to get them to come with us. We meet back at Caroline's. Call if anything goes wrong. Ready?"

Tricia and Mai nodded solemnly. Brent stole one of the half-eaten ojos de buey off the counter and popped it into his mouth.

"C'mon," he said. "My bike's locked in the front."

Leo had never stood on the back of a bike before. She had a bike, a small green hand-me-down from Belén with tassels on the handlebars, but she hadn't used it much since elementary school; it was currently in the garage with a cobweb-covered seat and flat tires. With the air rushing past her and ruffling her hair out of its braid, it was a little too cold for comfortable biking, and Leo found herself wishing she'd worn a heavier jacket, or that Brent was taller so he could block more wind. Still, they crossed downtown in seconds and turned from Main Street onto Rose Street to follow the glowing thread, and Leo began thinking that she should pull her bike out of its dusty retirement. This was way faster than walking.

"What happens if the path goes through a building or something?" Brent asked, shouting to be heard. "Do we go around? Will we lose the path, or will it recalculate like a GPS?"

"I don't know," Leo called back, leaning to speak into his ear and accidentally crashing her face into the hard shell of his helmet. She grimaced and leaned away, setting the bike wobbling as she shook her head.

"Watch out." Brent swayed but kept the bike upright. "What if the ghosts die—or disintegrate or whatever—before we get there? Will the path just disappear?"

"I don't know," Leo answered again. "That's not going to happen."

"How long before the special sight wears off?"

Brent asked next, swerving around the big pothole in front of the H-E-B that Daddy always forgot to avoid in his truck. "How long until the spirits disintegrate? Can Caroline do anything magical to keep it from happening?"

Leo was busy trying to keep her hair out of her mouth with one hand while keeping her balance on Brent's shoulder with the other. "I—*ack*—don't—*ptoo*—know!"

Brent was quiet while they slowed for a stop sign where Rose Street met Park Road. "You really have no idea what's going on, do you?"

As they coasted to a stop, the bike lurched through a deep puddle in the road, and Leo's left foot slipped off its step. She flailed and leaned, upsetting the balance of the bike, and jumped backward onto the street to avoid falling. She stumbled but stayed upright as Brent righted the bike and swerved to a full stop a few feet in front of her.

"Leo! Are you okay?"

"Yeah." She shook out her feet, which stung a little from standing on the narrow pegs and hitting the asphalt. "I'm fine."

"I'm sorry—I didn't see it. I should have given you my helmet; you're probably in the more dangerous position, statistically speaking." He unclipped his helmet and offered it to her. "I bet we're almost there anyways. Look at the trail."

Sure enough, the glowing gold light snaking down the street looked thicker and brighter than before.

Leo clipped the blue-and-green helmet under her chin and tilted it up off her forehead. Brent settled himself on the bike as she climbed back up on the pegs, holding Brent's shoulders a little more tightly this time.

"Ready?" Brent asked. Leo grunted a yes. They took off, and her stomach swooped even though Brent pedaled more slowly and steered more carefully this time.

"You know, I'm trying to learn," Leo said after her shoulders relaxed and her body settled into the cold rush of motion. "About magic, I mean. I study all the time, and I know a lot about the basics, sort of. Or . . . not a lot, but . . . I'm trying. It's just that things keep getting complicated. But I know some things."

Brent's light brown head of hair nodded. "I know. I'm the one who doesn't know anything about any of this. I never asked questions before because, well, it wasn't like my first experience with magic was all that great. And I thought magic was just your thing, and Caroline and I would still be, you know, muggles or whatever." He sighed and shrugged his shoulders. "But now, it's like you two have this whole new magical world of cool stuff to do and to learn, and I'm scared I'll be . . ."

"Left out," Leo finished for him. "I know. That's how I felt before. And Caroline too."

Brent's shoulders raised and lowered.

"We wouldn't do that," Leo said. "But I understand. Sometimes I listen to my sisters too much and do silly things and forget who my friends are. But Caroline wouldn't. And I won't either, anymore."

They biked up to Rose Hill Park, where Park Road got its name. Brent crossed the street to ride on the bike path surrounding the park, and they hit a patch of sunlight that warmed the back of Leo's neck.

Brent held his feet still, coasting on the reddish-brown gravel.

"Thanks," he said.

"Thank you," Leo replied. "You're helping me fix this mess."

"True," Brent said, and Leo could hear his self-satisfied smile even if she couldn't see it. "I am a pretty great friend, for a muggle."

Leo laughed. "Maybe," she said, "but you're not

the champion Ghostbuster anymore. Now we're tied!" She pointed over his shoulder to the park bench that was enveloped in an orangey-gold glow. In the middle, just visible if Leo squinted against the glare, sat Mayor Rose.

"No fair!" Brent stopped the bike, kicking up muddy gravel that bounced against Leo's ankles. "I was busy enjoying that moment." He waited for Leo to climb down before dismounting from his bike. "Besides, I should get at least half credit for providing transportation. And that makes me the undeniable champ, especially if you consider . . ."

Leo stopped listening to Brent's chatter as they approached Mayor Rose. He looked younger, like Abuela, but he also looked sadder, that wide grin absent from his face as he ripped leaves off the bush behind him and dropped them one by one onto the ground.

"Mayor Rose?" She jogged up to him and sat on the empty end of the bench. "What are you doing here?"

He sighed heavily and dropped a few more leaves before answering. "I used to run in these fields, back when they stretched out all the way to the county line," he said. "I came up with the idea for this park. The town was expanding fast, paving over more of the fields for new houses and buildings, and I wanted to keep some of the trees, the grass, where I played as a boy. It looks so different now. The whole town does."

"But . . . that's good, right?" Leo asked.

Mayor Rose just shrugged. "I always wanted the town to grow. Spent so much of my life pushing for it. I guess it's hard to accept that it may have outgrown me. It's the natural order of things, of course, but sometimes I look at the town and I worry that it's not in the right hands, that things are changing in the wrong way. I just wanted to make sure it got back on the right track."

Leo nodded. "I don't think you need to worry," she said. "We have two people and no animals running for mayor, and there's a lady at city hall who cares a lot about our political process. And she's teaching people about it." Brent rolled his bike up next to them. "And lots of people are interested. Like, Brent, did you know that mayors could make parks? Isn't that cool?"

"Uh . . . I guess?" Brent blinked at her.

"It's super cool," Leo insisted. "And probably they do lots of other important things. Like . . . like fix potholes!" She imagined Mayor Rose standing in front of a bulldozer, smoothing out the street while everyone in town gathered to clap. "No wonder you loved being mayor."

"The deadline to run for office passed," Mayor Rose said.

"I know." Leo patted his arm. "I went to city hall. I'm sorry I missed you. But I think this is for the best."

Mayor Rose sighed. "I probably should have left the campaign signs alone. But knowing that I have to let the town go on without me doesn't make it any easier."

Leo nodded.

"Anyway," Brent said, prodding Leo's elbow, "we do kind of need to get you back as soon as possible."

"I thought maybe I was going to stay here and become a poltergeist, haunting the park." Mayor Rose sighed dramatically.

"Oh no, you're not!" Brent exclaimed. "Not after everyone worked so hard to find you. We didn't chase you across town for you to disintegrate and ruin the park for everyone!"

Mayor Rose looked up at Brent for the first time. "How *did* you find me?" he asked. "And who are you, exactly?"

"He's my friend Brent," Leo explained. "And he's right. We've got teams out searching for all of you runaways, and we're not going to let any of you turn into restless ghosts. We're taking you back to the brujas who know how to fix this."

Mayor Rose dropped the last few leaves in his hand and looked at Leo with interest lighting his eyes. "Teams of search parties, huh? And a headquarters. And a plan once you have everyone back together again. Not bad. Whose idea was all this?"

"Leo's," Brent said. "We're all her friends. She called us together."

Mayor Rose nodded. "Exactly as I suspected. Seems like we have one passionate leader in Rose Hill's future, at least. That's good to know."

"Me?" Leo asked. "I wouldn't call this much of a plan. I just knew we had to fix everything before it got worse."

"An accurate description of a public servant." Mayor Rose grinned. "And rallying your friends to help you, that's not an easy task."

"Yeah." Leo shrugged. "But I'm not good at it. Nobody listens to me unless it's an emergency, and everyone is always annoyed with me, and I don't know what I'm doing most of the time."

Mayor Rose's laugh, high and clear, echoed through the park. "Spoken like a true politician," he said. He put his hands on his knees and grunted as he stood. "All right then, let's go. I wouldn't want to throw a wrench into your plan—taking a dip in credibility this early in your career could really hurt your chances down the line."

Chances for what? Leo thought. It was a funny thing to say. Leo, a leader? She was already going to be a baker and a bruja. Wasn't that enough jobs for one person?

But as they walked past the H-E-B, Leo couldn't help imagining that it was her standing in front of the bulldozer while the pothole got fixed once and for all. Maybe it would be cool to be a leader. She just had to figure out exactly what it meant.

Leo had shed her sweatshirt by the time they reached Caroline's house, the morning's chill burned mostly away by the noon sun. She was relieved to turn up Caroline and Brent's street, not only because Mayor Rose had even more dark hair mixed in with his white and gray. Plus, as they got close, their spirit vision showed several gold lines crisscrossing the street, which Leo took as a good sign.

"Hey, what happened?" Brent demanded as they passed his house. "Who's been messing around in my yard?"

His gate was open, and through it, huge fresh mounds of dirt had been dug up to make room for a bunch of large shrubs that hadn't stood there before.

"Uh-oh," Leo said. "Do you happen to know who owned the house before you?"

"Yeah, my mom's old cousin, Jack." Brent shrugged. "Why?"

Leo was saved from having to explain because, as they entered Caroline's front yard, the door burst open and Tricia and Mai ran out to greet them.

"I told you the trail was getting brighter," Tricia said. "They're here!"

"You made it." Mai smiled. "We ended up catching Old Jack in about ten minutes."

"Although we did have to help with a bit of unfinished business," Tricia held her hands close to Leo's face, showing off nails lined with fresh dirt and smelling like crumpled leaves.

"That was y'all in my yard?" Brent narrowed his eyes. "What did you do that for?"

"We were trying to get Old Jack to come inside," Mai explained. "But he wanted to finish planting, and he had already dug a bunch of holes anyway. We figured it would be worse to not fill them."

Brent looked unconvinced, but he shrugged and followed Tricia and Mai back into Caroline's house. "I guess I can tell my mom I had a . . . bolt of inspiration and planted them myself. Maybe it could be a good biology and ecology experiment."

"I saw my grandma!" Tricia whispered excitedly, pulling Leo back as the rest of the group entered the house. "She's really actually here. This is amazing."

Abuela and Mrs. Morales stood in the entryway, chatting with Mr. Nguyen, all their lines glowing bright orange.

"Where's Mr. Pérez?" Leo asked. "Did you find him?" She saw at least one or two golden trails stretching away from the living room, but with so many spirits together, it was hard to tell if it belonged to one of the spirits in the house.

"They found me," a voice called from the kitchen. Mr. Pérez smiled out the doorway. "I'm in here making eggs for some hungry gardeners."

"Yes!" Tricia and Mai skipped into the kitchen.

"Do the rest of you ghost hunters want some?" he asked.

"No, thank you," Leo said, at the same time Brent took off running toward the food, with Mayor Rose following him at a slower but no less enthusiastic pace.

"Is Mr. Pérez okay?" Leo whispered to Abuela. "He didn't get to finish what he came here for, did he?" She thought of how sad Mayor Rose had been before she had somehow convinced him that the future of

Rose Hill politics was secure. Mr. Pérez's cheeriness made Leo suspicious, like maybe he would try to run away again when no one was looking.

"He's fine," Mrs. Morales said. "Don't worry."

"But his sister moved away . . . ," Leo said.

"We found them at the public library," Abuela said.

"He planned to use the pay phones outside to call his sister, but we discovered they had all been removed since we were alive." Mrs. Morales shook her head. "Technology. But that's when a librarian found us outside, and after we told her what we were trying to do, she suggested we use the computers to send an email!"

Uh-oh. "You didn't let him, did you?" Leo asked. It would be bad enough to appear in front of a family member who knew you were a ghost. They could get upset, or scared. But at least they wouldn't have any proof. Sending an email would be evidence of magic that broke the boundary between life and death. Leo imagined news reporters and cameras flooding Rose Hill, strangers digging into everyone's business. There was a benefit to keeping the secret, at least from getting out to the whole entire world.

"Cálmate." Abuela put a hand on Leo's shoulder. "He didn't do it."

"He googled her instead," Mrs. Morales said. "She moved to Wisconsin with her wife. She writes poetry and publishes it online—he got to read some! She's happy. And that's all he really needed to know."

Leo leaned to look through the door of the kitchen. Mr. Pérez whistled as he scrambled eggs in the frying pan. "Good. That's good." She ticked spirits off on her fingers. Mr. Pérez, Old Jack, Mayor Rose, Mr. Nguyen, Mrs. Morales. Even Abuela, mostly. "That's everyone, isn't it?" she asked. "No more unfinished business?"

Abuela nodded. "I talked to your sister when we got here. Had to explain why a bunch of your little friends were showing up with spirits in tow. Now if only we can get back to el Otro Lado before we fade away, I'd say this was a pretty successful crossing of the veil."

Leo wasn't so sure about that. The spirits had caused an awful lot of trouble while they were here. But she was glad they wouldn't be sent back unhappy, wishing for more time to fix things. And this was what Caroline's magic was supposed to do.

Did that mean it was good they had crossed?

It was all too confusing, and Leo couldn't even begin to think about it until the spirits were out of danger. "Where is Caroline?" she asked. "How's the spell coming along?"

"Over here, Leo." Tía Paloma beckoned from the hallway. "We need to talk."

She looked stern, and Leo's stomach somersaulted as she remembered that, Abuela's pep talk aside, she hadn't asked her family's advice or permission before telling her friends about magic.

"Coming," she said, shooting a nervous look around the room. "Am I in trouble?" she whispered to Abuela.

Her grandmother shrugged, mischief dancing in her dark eyes. "One way to find out."

Leo groaned and walked into the dark hallway.

CHAPTER 16
A SECRET PROMISE

The smell of eggs and the glow of golden light faded as Leo entered the hallway, replaced by the sharp scent of herbs she should probably recognize and the flickering of candles. She followed her nose into Caroline's room, where Isabel sat cross-legged on the bed, a thick book in her lap and a frown on her face. Brown candles—for understanding, research, concentration—clustered on top of the dresser.

"Um, hi," Leo said. "How's it going?"

Caroline's face popped up from behind the bed like a prairie dog. Her bangs stuck to her forehead, and a crease stayed between her eyes even as her mouth tilted into an almost-smile.

"Hi, Leo. I think your aunt wanted you next door. We're kind of busy, planning the portal-opening spell."

Leo nodded, looking from her friend to her sister to the thick fog of burning rosemary for more concentration and clarity. "You've figured it out, though?" she asked. "You're going to be able to start soon?"

Isabel looked up from her book, scowling. "We're doing our best, Leo. There isn't a whole lot of information on how to open a portal to el Otro Lado, because it's a terribly dangerous thing to do! We're trying to isolate the part that opens the veil without dealing with the really nasty spirit-summoning parts, but most of the books we really need are restricted by the Southwest Regional Brujería and Spellcraft Association. Would you please just go find Tía Paloma? I think she has a project for you; she's been acting weird."

"Okay, okay." Leo held up her hands and continued down the hall. "Tía Paloma?"

"In here," a voice called, though it didn't sound like her tía. Leo followed it to the TV room, which used to be Mr. and Mrs. Campbell's bedroom before all the changes. Tía Paloma sat facing Leo on the couch in the center of the room. All the lights were off, and two tiny votive candles sat in the middle of the carpet, flames dancing and reflecting in Tía Paloma's eyes until they looked almost as white as the candle wax. Leo rubbed her eyes. In the dim light, the orange trails of all the spirits crisscrossed brightly across her vision, wiggling as their owners moved around the house. One trail even looked like it led straight to Tía Paloma, but that couldn't be right—her aunt wasn't a spirit.

"Close the door, please," Tía Paloma said. Her voice still sounded odd, flat and empty of feeling. Leo knew her aunt's anger, how it escaped in wild hand gestures and restless movement and fast sentences. She didn't recognize this emptiness.

"Is everything okay?" she asked. "Is this about my friends? I had a good reason to tell them—"

"Leo Logroño," Tía Paloma said. "I need to tell you something very important."

"You do?" Leo cocked her head, trying to see past the flickering candles to make sense of her aunt's behavior.

Once Leo had signed Tía Paloma's birthday card as "Leo Logroño" and her family had laughed at her for the rest of the night. "Believe me," Tía Paloma had said, "I know which Leo you are." So why was she using Leo's last name to address her now?

“First I need your promise.” Tía Paloma held up one hand. “You have to agree that you won’t tell Caroline. Swear it.”

Leo’s mouth flew open and her eyebrows arched. “What? No! Caroline is part of this. She deserves to know everything that’s going on—she has to know, so she can fix it all. Besides, I’m not keeping secrets from my friends anymore. Abuela even said I don’t have to. And you’re acting really weird. You should just tell me whatever it is so that we can all work it out together!”

Instead of getting angry or arguing, Tía Paloma stared straight ahead, the corners of her mouth lifting into just the hint of a smile.

“You’re a good friend,” she said. “But will you give me a chance to explain, at least? Promise you’ll hear me out—all the way out—before you call Caroline in here?”

Leo hesitated. This whole conversation was wrong, and she felt like she was missing the meaning of everything Tía Paloma said. She searched her aunt’s words for some trick or trap, but when she couldn’t find one, she eventually shrugged. “Okay, I guess. What do you have to tell me?”

Tía Paloma’s smile went slack. Something shimmered in the air around her, and the orange trail closest to her pulsed. A figure rose from behind the couch, standing up so that its face loomed above Tía Paloma's. It was a face Leo recognized, even if she hadn't seen it in more than a year. The woman was younger now, about the age she was in the picture frame next to Caroline's bed. She had the same round cheeks as Caroline, and the same pointed chin.

Mrs. Campbell was the seventh spirit.

"Caroline!" Leo hissed, her promise forgotten in an instant. Her shocked voice didn't reach above a whisper, so she cleared her throat to try again.

"Leo, please." Tía Paloma and Mrs. Campbell both spoke, their hands rising at the same time to reach for her. "You promised."

"This doesn't make sense," Leo said. "You're here, but you didn't tell anyone? Caroline started this whole spell for you and you just—don't you want to see her?" She watched Mrs. Campbell's face fall, the sadness mirrored in Tía Paloma's expression. "And what did you do to my tía?"

"I'm sorry," Mrs. Campbell said. Tía Paloma spoke along with the spirit and held out one hand, mimicking her gesture. "I know I have a lot to answer, but I can explain everything. First of all, your aunt is fine. She's just channeling me, which creates a unique effect when I also exist on the corporeal plane."

"Um." Leo tilted her head. Mrs. Campbell, like Caroline, talked like she had swallowed a dictionary. "Okay." Leo had seen Alma and Belén channel ghosts before, speaking for them in the messenger tent on Día de los Muertos. Tía Paloma might get worn out if she channeled a spirit for too long, but she would recover just fine. "But why is she channeling you?"

Tía Paloma and Mrs. Campbell sighed. "Caroline told her that there might still be one more spirit running around here in the world of the living. Your aunt cast a spell to connect with that spirit, using her own birth talent. It started to work, and she was about to discover that I was here hiding and I . . . well, I panicked. I possessed her so that she couldn't give me away. It seems that possession works equally well whether the spirit is incorporeal—without a body—or corporeal."

Leo frowned. "But you're going to let her go, right? You have to."

"Of course." Mrs. Campbell and Tía Paloma pressed their hands to their hearts. "I'm not trying to harm her, I just needed a chance to explain myself. But now I'm explaining everything all wrong."

The tightness in Leo's chest settled a little. She understood Mrs. Campbell's rushed, muddled explanation. She even understood doing something a little bit wrong when you were scared of getting caught. And this was Caroline's mom, who had made Leo pancakes after her first-ever sleepover and driven her home from countless playdates, parties, and swim lessons. She wasn't scary, or evil, or trying to hurt anyone. She was nervous and confused, like all the spirits. Like everyone was today.

Leo sat down on the side of the couch that wrapped sideways so that she could see both dark-haired women. "Okay," she said. "It's okay. Just tell me why you're hiding."

Two sets of shoulders sagged in relief. "I was pulled through the veil a few minutes after midnight last night," Mrs. Campbell explained. "And although I didn't know what was happening exactly, I had a decent theory. Caroline told you about my family magic, after all. I'd heard all the stories, even if I didn't believe them completely. And I'd just seen Caroline light the candle before going to bed. So it wasn't too much of a leap to assume that she had inadvertently brought me back."

"You saw her?" Leo asked. "How?"

Mrs. Campbell wrapped one hand around the

opposite wrist, twisting the silver bracelet she wore. "I watch her," she said, "from el Otro Lado. She was upset, and I like to be there when she's having a hard time. I know I can't really help her, but . . ."

Leo nodded.

"At any rate"—Mrs. Campbell cleared her throat—"I've heard enough family lore to know the dangers of bringing spirits back to the realm of the living. It's not just a problem for us, you know; the living spell casters who try it often suffer adverse effects. These spells can go wrong in so many ways and hurt the caster, but even if they go right . . . it takes a mental toll. Especially for a loved one, especially for someone who's still grieving. So I knew I couldn't let Caroline or my husband know I was here."

"Why?" Leo asked, her jaw clenching stubbornly. "She would be happy to see you. My family sends messages back and forth for people who have lost loved ones, and it never hurts anybody."

Mrs. Campbell shook her head. "Your family is careful about their messages. It happens only once a year, only for the span of a few minutes, and only for spirits who have been gone long enough for their loved ones to heal. It's a comforting moment, not a total reversal of the boundary between life and death."

Leo clicked her tongue. The boundary again. "I

don't get why you care more about the importance of some magical boundary than you do about your daughter," she snapped. "But I know that my mamá would never hide away and leave me to figure out dangerous magic by myself. She would help me." It wasn't a nice thing to say, but Leo didn't feel like being nice.

She noticed the tears on Tía Paloma's cheeks first, the twin tracks catching the light of the candle flames. Her stomach curled in on itself as Mrs. Campbell sniffed and wiped her face, but she held her chin high. "I didn't mean . . . I just think you're worried about the wrong thing," Leo said. "If you'll just let me go get Caroline, she can tell you that she's not going to have any mental toll. She wants to see you."

"She always wants to see me," Mrs. Campbell whispered. "She woke up every day for months, and it was the first thing she'd say, even before she opened her eyes. She would wish for it to be a dream. That it never happened. She didn't want to accept it; she still doesn't—that's why she cast the spell."

"She cast the spell so she could see you again," Leo said. "So she could feel better."

"It's not about feeling better," Mrs. Campbell

argued. "If Caroline sees me now, then all the progress of the past months—the friendships she's rebuilt with you and Brent, the new home she and her father have made, her interest in her schoolwork—all of that will be shaken. She'll be back to wishing for a life she can't have, for all the things I can't give her."

Leo dropped her eyes to her toes, sadness prickling the back of her throat. "She might think it's worth it," she said.

"She might," Mrs. Campbell agreed. "I don't."

Leo watched the white candle flicker in its shallow tin, almost all liquid by now, its wick standing upright in the clear puddle. Being sad and angry at the unfairness of life and death wouldn't help Mrs. Campbell, or any of the spirits, and most important, it wouldn't help Caroline. She blinked and swallowed until the threat of tears retreated.

"Okay," she said softly. "Okay. So that's why you hid."

"That's why I hid." Mrs. Campbell nodded. "I didn't realize that while I hid, the candle was still burning, pulling others across the veil. I only figured it out when I saw Mayor Rose wandering down the street, hours later."

Leo's eyes widened. "You sent him to Caroline,"

she said. "That's why he and the other spirits knocked on the door."

"I told him to wake her up and tell her that he had crossed the veil," Mrs. Campbell said. "I thought she would blow out the candle, and that would be enough to end the effects of the spell. Then I thought we might need to gather all the spirits together, so I intercepted Mr. Nguyen and Mr. Pérez. And when that didn't work . . . I tried to help as much as I could, although I didn't realize just how complicated the spell was or how much work it would take to undo it."

Leo worked her way down a mental checklist of small mysteries. "The board game pieces," she said. "The phone calls."

"Caroline got all the information she needed." Mrs. Campbell's smile was small but proud. "She barely needed my help. I have no doubt she'll figure out how to send everyone back, and soon. But . . ."

"She doesn't know she's sending you too." Leo's toe scratched lines into the carpet.

"She can't know," Mrs. Campbell said. "Leo, please say you understand. I need your help if I'm going to pull this off."

Leo didn't answer right away. She was thinking about secrets. Why her family kept so many of them, and why it bothered her so much when they did. She hated when her older sisters babied her, made decisions that they thought were for her own good that really just kept her feeling frustrated and confused. She didn't want to keep Caroline in the dark.

But even more than that, she didn't want to do anything to hurt her.

"What do you need me to do?"

Mrs. Campbell's face relaxed. "I think a distraction should be enough. They're doing a portal spell, so I'll need to slip through unnoticed once the portal is opened. It will be good to tell your aunt as well, so she can take the number of spirits into account when planning." Mrs. Campbell twisted her hands together. "I have to let her go, of course. She won't remember the details of this conversation, but she'll know what happened. She'll be tired, disoriented. That's another reason I need your help."

Leo nodded. "I'll make sure she doesn't tell Caroline, even by accident," she said. "Don't worry. She'll understand."

"Thank you," Mrs. Campbell said. "I have one last thing to organize, but I can handle that myself, and then I'll go back to hiding in the yard where it's not so crowded. I'll wait for your distraction when the portal opens."

"I'll do something dramatic," Leo promised.

Mrs. Campbell smiled. "I'm glad Caroline has you as a friend." She hesitated. "Watch out for her? The spells they're looking at, opening portals to other realms, they can be volatile."

"Of course," Leo said, making a mental note to look up that word too. "My family will make sure she's okay."

Mrs. Campbell nodded. She closed her eyes, let out a long breath. Tía Paloma blinked and took a shuddering breath on her own while Mrs. Campbell watched, biting the nail of her thumb.

"I'm sorry," Mrs. Campbell said softly, bracing Tía Paloma as she tilted sideways. "You're okay."

"Tía Paloma?" Leo asked. "Do you need anything?"

Tía Paloma groped around the top of her head until she found her glasses and pushed them down over her eyes. "Leo? What happened? There's another spirit loose, and we need to . . ." She turned her head toward Mrs. Campbell, but the spirit had already ducked and disappeared into the shadows of the room.

"We found the other spirit," Leo told her, "but we have to keep it a secret for right now. But everything's going to be fine."

"Okay. Good." Tía Paloma rolled her eyes all the way back in her head and massaged her temples. "In that case, do we have any water? And something to eat."

Once Tía Paloma had been brought up to speed, fed a large plate of eggs (Leo added a big pile of cheese on top, in true Logroño style), and sworn to secrecy, they joined Isabel and Caroline in the bedroom. The brown candles were out and the lights were on, and Caroline met Leo with a wide and only slightly exhausted-looking grin.

"We think we have it," she said. "The basic concept, anyway." Caroline wiped her bangs off her forehead and brandished a piece of notebook paper filled with scribbles and scratch outs and a sketched round shape with tiny notes written all around it.

Leo beamed. "That's amazing." She remembered how scary it was to invent a spell, the uncertainty of making decisions you barely understood. "So should we get started?"

Caroline nodded. "We don't know exactly how much time the spirits have, but my dad's been leaving work early this week, so we have to be fast."

"It's not quite that easy," Isabel said, sighing. "We need a lot of ingredients and relics, and we have to prepare everything just right. I already sent Alma and Belén a list, but we still have to roll each candle and . . ." She sat heavily on the bed. "We can't use Abuela or the spirits to help, either, because their energy is from the wrong side of the veil and won't work right."

"Well." Leo looked from her sister to her aunt. "We have a lot of other helpers here who aren't spirits."

Isabel looked at her like she had just suggested that Señor Gato could wash the dishes. "Your friends? Leo, don't be silly."

"It's not a bad idea," Tía Paloma mused. "Magical ability isn't needed for most of the preparation."

"Really?" Isabel asked. "Tía Paloma, they're sixth graders! Isn't it bad enough she got them involved in the first place?"

Leo winced. She had worried what her family would think and imagined what they would say. But Tía Paloma was the one to speak first.

"They're a good group of kids," she said with a hard look at Isabel. "When I was your age, two of my best friends didn't even believe me when I told them I was a bruja, and the one who did would never have helped me with my . . . well, she used to call it my 'freak stuff.'"

Isabel glowered. "You told people too?"

Tía Paloma sighed. "Everyone tells someone, my

dear. Marisol's on her third or fourth boyfriend; so far, none of them have taken it that well."

"She never told me that she . . ." Isabel frowned at the hallway carpet. "I've never told anyone."

"Well, you do take rules so seriously." Tía Paloma patted Isabel's arm.

"Didn't Abuela talk to you?" Leo asked Isabel. "Didn't she tell you"—She tried to remember Abuela's words—"that magic should strengthen relationships instead of ruining them?" It didn't sound as inspiring when she said it.

"I guess." Isabel still scowled. "She told me to stop giving you bad advice, but I'm only telling you what everyone always told me."

"Isabel," Tía Paloma said. "You were the first girl to turn fifteen. We needed you to keep the secret from your sisters until they were old enough to learn, and we wanted to protect you from the pain we sometimes felt. People aren't always kind to others they see as different—high schoolers least of all. It seemed like a good rule at the time, to keep things under wraps until your sisters got older. I'm sure your mother never meant to cut you off from your friends."

"It doesn't matter," Isabel said, in what was a shockingly good impersonation of a sulky Marisol.

"I didn't have any in the first place."

"Don't be upset right now, Isabel," Caroline said softly. "Be upset later, after you save the day."

"Yeah." Leo nodded. "You can yell at me for a whole week for all the mistakes I've made, once we get the spirits back where they belong. I won't even tell Mamá."

Isabel groaned. She still didn't look happy, but she held up her hands. "Fine, whatever. If you want to let them help, they can help. It's Tricia and Mai who are here?"

"And Brent," Leo said.

"Brent is here?" Caroline's face turned three shades of pink. "Did you tell him . . . what I did?"

"Um, yeah." Leo hadn't thought much about the fact that sharing her secret also meant sharing Caroline's without her permission. "It sort of came up. Sorry."

"No, it's okay. I'm glad, I think. Now that people know, it's like it's official." She nodded at Leo, smiling. "And I'm about to reverse a spell, just like you. I'm really a bruja, I guess. Unless I totally ruin it."

"You're going to do perfectly," Leo told her friend, locking eyes with Caroline and using her most serious-business voice. When she had started her first reversal spell, Caroline's confidence had given her courage. "I know it."

Caroline looked down at her pajamas, swiped her sticky bangs off her forehead. "If a bunch of people are here, maybe I should change. I'll meet you out there." Caroline turned to her closet and started pulling out shirts, leaving Isabel, Tía Paloma, and Leo to back into the hallway and close the door.

"Isabel . . . ," Leo started.

"No, don't." Isabel ruffled the top of Leo's head. "I'm being a jerk. It's like Tía Paloma said. You have good friends. And today, we're lucky you do."

"Right," Tía Paloma said, clapping her hands together. "And let's hope they're good workers too, because we have enough for a whole bruja convention to do, and not much time to do it. Alma and Belén will be here any minute—let's inspect our troops."

CHAPTER 17

SPELLCRAFT

"We're following this outline to form the gate," Isabel explained, holding up the sketch she and Caroline had made, a ring of candles connected by dotted lines of sprinkled herbs, salt, and sugar. "We can handle the arrangement, but each candle needs to be prepared before we can start. Cleansed, carved, and rubbed with oil and spices—oh, and we'll need to chop up at least a few of the herbs fresh, because we don't want to take chances with stale ingredients."

"Sounds like a sandwich," Brent whispered. "Speaking of which, Caroline, you don't have any peanut butter and jelly around here, do you? Somebody really failed to follow through on her promise of pastries."

He sat across the Campbells' dining-room table from Isabel, with Tricia and Mai on one side and Leo on the other. Leo kicked his foot under the table, but Isabel had already stopped to frown at him.

"Time is against us here, but more important than speed is intention. You can't simply follow the directions; you have to put your heart and your will into it. If you think this is some big joke"—her eyes turned steely as they focused on Brent—"then you'd better go home now. You're endangering the work the rest of us are doing."

"Yes, ma'am." Brent ducked his head. "Sorry, ma'am. I don't think it's a joke."

Mai raised her hand, like they were in school, which made Leo want to laugh (although she didn't dare risk the death glare Isabel would give her if she did).

"Um, is it okay if I just help with chopping the herbs?" Mai asked. "I'm not sure how my mom would feel about me doing witchcraft."

Leo opened her mouth to ask what she meant by that, but Isabel spoke first.

"Of course, Mai. You don't have to do anything

you're not comfortable with."

"But I do want to help," Mai said quickly, smiling at Leo. "And I cut herbs and vegetables all the time at home. It's not magic, but it's a useful culinary skill."

"I think I'd be good at the cleansing part," Brent volunteered. "My mom does a lot of juice cleanses, and they're actually tasty sometimes."

Leo leaned her elbows on the table and buried her head in her hands.

"I don't think it's that kind of cleanse," Tricia hissed. "It's probably like, magical cleansing, right?"

"We're using smoke," Isabel said, "since the original spell and Caroline's magic is all fire based. Sage smoke, to free the candles of any previous magical contamination."

"Even better," Brent said. "I love burning stuff!" He paused, glanced around the table, and grimaced. "Okay, I'm sorry. I promise I'll stop messing around if you let me help."

Abuela, who had been banished to the living room with the rest of the spirits and Mr. Campbell's bag of adult coloring books, poked her head into the dining room. The golden glow of her trail had faded almost completely as the spell from the ojos de buey wore off.

"Are you using rosemary or dragon's-blood oil to

prepare the candles?" she asked. "You know, when I was young, no one could dress a candle like I could—"

"Abuela, we told you, no spirits." Isabel sighed. "Your magic is different now. It will mess with the spell. Plus, working magic might make you disintegrate faster!"

"So—what? I can't even hear what ingredients you're using?" Abuela frowned. "I'm the one you're going to push through this gate you're creating—I just want to know how it's being made."

"It's going to be fine," Isabel growled. "We don't need any advice."

"I mean . . . I might need some advice," Tricia spoke up. "I don't know what I'm doing, and I don't want to mess it up if my grandma's afterlife is at stake."

"See?" Abuela beamed. "Smart girl."

"Mami, are you bothering Isabel?" Tía Paloma leaned out of the kitchen doorway with her hands full of the contents of the Campbell pantry, which she was raiding for anything that looked useful. "Go back to your coloring."

"I was only offering." Abuela pouted, her face young enough that for a moment she could have been the long-haired, sweater-wearing twin of Mamá.

"Abuela, enough," Isabel sighed. "I have too many

headaches to deal with already."

"Is she talking about us?" Brent fake-whispered, loud enough to be heard all through the house. "That seems uncalled for."

Tricia shushed him, and Mai defended him, and Abuela kept arguing with Isabel until Caroline joined the gathering to see what the commotion was. Leo felt the energy and purpose in the room splintering, stirring, swirling into a mess that would soon be too big to clean up.

"Hey!" Her voice got lost in the general muttering. "Hey!" She had never needed a big silver coach's whistle so badly. "Would y'all *listen up*?"

Her friends and family settled like a flock of birds on a telephone wire, and Leo knew they were only one squawk or squabble away from starting up again.

"Look, we need to be ready to start as soon as the ingredients arrive," she said. Isabel opened her mouth, but Leo pushed on. "We have a good plan. Mai will chop, Brent will cleanse. Tricia and I can prepare candles, and Abuela can supervise us. *Just supervise.*" She held out a warning finger to Abuela. "No touching. Pretend you're still in . . . cor . . . por . . . um . . ."

"Incorporeal," Caroline offered.

Leo clicked her tongue but smiled at her friend.

"Yeah, that. Pretend you still have no body. Caroline and Isabel will set everything in place and light the candles. Tía Paloma will make sure everyone is doing their job right, and troubleshoot. Oh, and the rest of the spirits will color until we're ready for them. Does that sound like a plan?"

Abuela nodded. Brent, Tricia, and Mai nodded. Tía Paloma had a funny smile on, like she was watching one of those reality show YouTube clips where the quiet old lady in slippers suddenly sings the best opera anyone's ever heard—but she nodded. Isabel shrugged. "That's basically what I said."

"Great," Tía Paloma said. "Caroline, does your dad have some old newspapers? It's good to lay them down wherever you're setting up the candle ring. You don't want to be cleaning wax off hardwood floors."

As Isabel set up Leo's friends in different parts of the kitchen, Leo saw Mayor Rose, his hair dark brown and his face unwrinkled, looking at her from his seat in the living room. He winked at Leo and gave her a thumbs-up with a hand full of colored pencils.

By the time Alma and Belén knocked on the front door, the whole Campbell house had transformed into a bruja workshop.

"So we want this symbol carved on each candle," Isabel explained to Leo and Tricia as they smoothed cling wrap over the wooden kitchen table to protect it from oil and herbs and candle wax. "It's like an upside-down U, see? And then the rosemary oil gets rubbed in."

"You want to start at the middle and rub the oil up to the top," Abuela added, "since you're sending us away, not drawing us closer. And keep that in your head too. You want to open a door for us to return to el Otro Lado. Concentrate on that."

Leo watched Brent drop a burning bundle of sage into the sink and scramble to pick it back up. At the counter, Mai sneezed and scattered chopped lemongrass across the floor, mixing with the marigold petals. Panic squeezed Leo's throat shut, and she fought the urge to throw up her hands and tell everyone to stop, that her friends should go home now because this had all been a big mistake.

"Intention," Abuela whispered to her as Alma dropped two cleansed candles on the table between Leo and Tricia, and Belén handed Brent two new ones. Leo swallowed and nodded. She couldn't do her job while she worried about everyone else's. She closed her eyes and took one long breath in and out.

Her candle was tall and yellow, thin enough to fit

in a candlestick and be used to decorate a fancy dinner table. According to Isabel's sketch, there would be three candles like this, three of the fatter yellow candles that stood on their own, and one white candle in glass. Yellow for the dead, the same color Caroline had used in her spell. Two different types used together to bring together the two different worlds. White to unite all the complicated different parts of the spell, as well as all the different spell casters. To purify all their intentions, to focus them on the goal. To open the gate. Would one white candle be strong enough to do all that?

Intention. She scratched the doorway symbol into the thick end of the candle with the pointy end of a dried-up pen from Caroline's junk drawer. She tried to focus on that curved shape in the yellow wax. She needed to think about doorways? Was that right? If she looked out the kitchen doorway, she could see into the living room where the spirits milled around, comparing coloring pages and craning their necks to see how the spell was going. They were starting to look so young that they could have been a group of high schoolers loitering at the Dairy Queen on the interstate.

If the spell didn't work, would they eventually have a room full of baby spirits?

Focus, Leo told herself. She dripped oil onto her candle and breathed in the rosemary smell. *Think of opening el Otro Lado. Think of doors.*

Her mind found the swinging blue doors of the bakery. They opened in both directions, in and out, so that you could always push through if your hands were full. There was a chip on the bottom of the left door where Leo had crashed once when she was little while running away from Alma and Belén in some game, knocking out a baby tooth. The doors kept the front of the bakery—where the customers were—away from the back, where you could be angry or tired or a bruja or whatever you wanted.

She thought about boundaries, how they separated loved ones but kept the spirits safe. How breaking them could be happy and heartbreaking. She thought of everything that had been gained by the spirits coming through the veil, and everything that might still be lost. The rosemary smell picked up a hint of spice as Leo settled into the quiet area of her mind where her magic came from. She forgot about the rest of her friends, about the long day of confusion and worry. When she focused on a spell, she wasn't worried or confused or stressed or embarrassed. She wasn't a baby sister or a mess maker or a secret teller or a young leader. She was Leo. She was a bruja. And she had a job to do.

When they had finished, Leo carried the candles to Caroline and Isabel. She knelt on the living-room rug where Alma and Belén had settled in to watch the excitement. Caroline set the candles up in their spiral pattern, with the white veladora in the center. Mai passed Caroline a bag of fresh lemongrass, which Caroline sprinkled in a circle around the outside of the arrangement while Isabel sprinkled an intricate spiral design between the candles in brown sugar.

"How will we know if it's working?" Brent whispered on Leo's right. Leo shrugged. Aside from the smell of magic that lingered in her nose, her only hint that the spell was working would show up when the candles were lit.

Isabel looked at the setup, glanced at her sketched paper, and then stood up and put her hands on her hips. "What do you think?" she asked Caroline. "We're not summoning a guide, so it looks a lot simpler than the picture, but that's good, I think. It's less chance for things to go spectacularly wrong. And it's closer to how you started the spell, just one candle." Isabel's words tumbled out fast, betraying her nervousness. "Anyway, you're the primary caster, so it's up to you to say when it's ready. . . . So what do you think?"

Caroline's hazel eyes flicked nervously around

the room like a mouse caught by a cat. Leo met her friend's gaze, smiled encouragingly, and winked. *You can do this,* she thought loud and clear in her head.

Caroline drew herself up to her full stand-up-straight height, which was almost as tall as Isabel. She nodded. "It feels right," she said. "Let's light it up before we lose any more time."

"I'll get everyone!" Alma jumped to her feet and darted into the dining room, where a few of the spirits were still coloring. Those who had already been watching inched closer to the portal spell. Leo's magical sight had worn off, and she could no longer see the spirits' glowing lights, so she could only hope that Mrs. Campbell was somewhere nearby, hiding.

When the living room was crowded with the living and the dead, Isabel took Brent's long-necked lighter and handed it to Caroline. Leo held her breath as Caroline pointed the flame toward the wick of the white center candle.

One heartbeat passed. Two. Three.

The wick caught, and the hum of the air conditioning cut off, along with all the lights in the house. Mai squeaked, Caroline blinked at her hand, and Leo grinned in relief. Caroline's magic was real, and it was working.

Caroline lit the rest of the candles, working her way out from the center. Bent over the newspaper-lined altar, her face glowed with orange light and gray shadows, and her tall frame pulled inward with the same focused energy she had when taking a test at school. She spun a plastic ring around the finger of her free hand, and her hunched shoulders and twitchy movements made her look like a candle flame herself—bright and burning and full of power.

She was a bruja.

The last candle caught the flame. Caroline leaned back on her heels. There was a flurry of rustling as everyone in the room shifted at the same time, glancing around at each other.

Brent said, "So now wh—"

That was when the altar exploded.

The crack was lightning and the crash was thunder and the wind spat orange petals into Leo's eyes and mouth as she scrambled back and tripped against someone else. By the time she and Tricia untangled themselves, the wind had died and the petals were settling slowly, all the candles knocked over and doused, the protective newspapers crumpled and scattering herbs, salt, and sugar across the floorboards.

In place of the ruined altar, a glowing cross-hatch

of orange, turquoise, pink, and red lights traced the patterns Isabel had sketched. Two columns of light rose up to the ceiling, and the air between them shimmered like a waterfall of glass or clear liquid silk. It almost hurt Leo's eyes to look at the blur. She wanted to touch it.

"Is that . . . what's supposed to happen?" Brent asked.

Leo stepped toward the veil. Tricia put a hand on her elbow, but she shook it off and took another step toward the inviting colors.

"It's . . . ," Belén said. "It wasn't . . . I'm not sure."

"Do you think something went wrong?" Mai asked. "Maybe I messed it up by being nervous."

"Maybe I messed it up by being hungry," Brent piped up. "Ow! Cut it out."

"Tía Paloma? What do you think?" Isabel asked. She gathered her sheets of drawings and ingredient lists and sat on the couch.

Leo stepped into the circle of light, feet passing through the colorful design just like the golden spirit trails.

"I don't think this was the expected result," Tía Paloma said. "I'm sorry, kids, I don't blame any of you, but I think we should maybe try again, have just the brujas help this time. We'll hope that will solve whatever— Leo, what are you doing?"

Leo heard her aunt's voice, but her fingers were just inches away from the veil, and the urge to brush her skin against the shine was too strong to stop. It felt cold and fluid, and it tickled the roof of Leo's mouth, like allergies. Without thinking, she plunged her hand through up to the elbow.

"Leo!" Isabel jumped up from the couch, scattering papers and petals in every direction.

"Whoa whoa whoa!" Brent windmilled his arms and then wrapped them around his torso like he was wearing a straitjacket.

Leo drew her arm back. "What?" she said, finding her voice with only a little bit of difficulty in the buzzing excitement flowing through her body. "It doesn't hurt."

"Your arm disappeared!" Alma said, words tripping over Belén, who said the same thing.

"Leo?" It was Abuela who took a step closer when everyone else was shrinking away. "What are you seeing?"

Leo turned back to the tall, glowing, shining gate. "Are y'all telling me you're *not* seeing this?"

CHAPTER 18

THE GATE

"It's right there," Leo said. "There's a gate with a veil in the middle, and I'm pretty sure it leads to el Otro Lado. And it's *glowing*. How are y'all missing it?"

"How are you missing that it might not be a great idea to stick your hand into an actual gateway to death?" Tricia responded, eyes wide. Mai nodded along, and Brent shuddered.

"It's the veil," Leo said. "The spirits have already passed through it twice, and they're fine. It's not going to hurt anyone."

"I think you're forgetting that the first time they passed through it, they died," Brent muttered.

"Could this be a side effect of the ojos de buey?" Caroline asked. "I never saw those glowing orange trails everyone was talking about either."

"But none of us see what Leo sees," Tricia said.

"Brent ate the most of the muffins, so he should be the one with lingering side effects," Mai added.

Leo tapped her foot. "Can we figure out the why later? The portal is open, so we should be getting the spirits through as fast as we can." She would have thought her friends and family could stay focused on their time-sensitive issue instead of getting distracted by their inability to see something shiny.

"Do you think they should just . . ." Caroline waved her hand in the general direction of the gate. "Walk into it?"

"Why not?" Leo asked. "That was the plan, right?"

"Of course." Abuela nodded. "If Leo sees a portal that the rest of us can't see, then the portal spell worked."

"Yeah," Isabel said, "but how do we know the portal goes where we want it to?"

"Once the first person goes through, they can tell us how it is," Belén said.

Alma nodded. "Or at least, they can tell us if it sends them back to being normal ghosts."

The twins shared a worried glance. "But what if it's not—"

"If you don't mind," Mayor Rose spoke up, "I'm happy to try it out. I'm feeling quite tired, and I'm ready to let the town go on without me." He walked up to the center of the carpet, his feet tangled in the glowing patterns, half a step from plunging straight through the veil. "Here?" he asked Leo, who nodded. "Well then, it has been a true pleasure and honor meeting all of you. It may seem a small thing, but the courage and creativity shown here today has given one old soul hope for the future of Rose Hill, of Texas, of the world. Sincerest farewells, friends and fellow citizens." With one last flash of his brilliant smile, he stepped forward.

And stepped forward again. And again, passing entirely through the veil and out the other side without creating so much as a ripple along its surface.

"Hmm." He glanced at Leo. "Did I miss it?"

Leo shook her head, frowning. "You went right into it," she said. "You didn't feel anything?"

Mayor Rose shrugged. Mr. Pérez stepped up to the gate, waved his hands out in front of him. "There's nothing here," he said.

"But there is!" Leo marched up next to him and stuck her arm into the gate, feeling unreasonably relieved by the surge of cold energy and the wide eyes of her friends and family. "See?"

"Maybe you have to be able to see it to use it?" Abuela mused. "But that doesn't help us if we don't know why Leo can see it and the rest of us can't."

"We could run back to the bakery for the leftover ojos de buey," Tricia suggested.

"No, we'd have to make a new batch," Alma said. "Those were to find spirits, not spirit doors."

"Besides, do we know if the gate will stay open long enough for us to get there and back?" Caroline asked.

"We don't really know anything for sure," Isabel said, her mouth pressed together in frustration.

"It wouldn't work," Tía Paloma said. The finality of her voice carried through the room despite its low volume. "They need a guide."

"A guide?" Isabel shook her head slowly. "We saw that in the portal spells we looked up. You told us we shouldn't use that part of the spell."

"We shouldn't." Tía Paloma sighed into her hands. "It would be . . . that's the reason portal spells are so dangerous, why no ethical resource will describe them in full. The kind of creatures you need, ones who can walk between worlds . . . they're full of power and often unpleasant. Attracting the attention of one is the last thing a wise bruja should be doing."

"I don't understand." Isabel shook her head again. "If you knew this would happen, why did you let us cast the spell? Why bother with any of it?"

"I hoped the spirits could cross on their own!" Tía Paloma was almost shouting now. "They all belong in el Otro Lado, so I thought they might be able to pass."

"It worked once," Caroline said. "I pulled them through already."

Tía Paloma shook her head. "That's different," she said. "You were pulling them here. You were the guide. To get them back, we need someone pulling from over there."

"So let's summon someone," Isabel said, reaching for one of her papers and pulling a pen out from her pocket. "We'll put the pentacle back in, and we'll get someone here who can guide them, and then—"

"Absolutely not." Abuela grabbed the paper from Isabel's hand, her voice calm but her motion quick and definite. "You are not doing this, Isabel Lucero."

"Abuela, you're being—"

"No." Abuela's eyes were hard and fierce. "I lost my Isabel to a spell like this. I'm not letting you repeat her mistake."

The room of fifteen humans and spirits fell silent.

Leo remembered the sticker-covered door to Tía Isabel's room, heard the sad emptiness of Tía Paloma's knock.

"I thought she had an accident," Leo said, turning to Tía Paloma.

"A magical accident," Belén answered when Tía Paloma didn't speak. "She wanted to understand more about how our birth-order powers came to be, and she thought they were related to el Otro Lado. She kept experimenting, trying to see if she could make her power stronger. She wanted answers so badly, she didn't care about the risk."

"I didn't know," Isabel whispered. "Nobody told me."

"Marisol told us," Alma whispered. "After that time Belén fainted when we were trying to break the record for longest channeling. She said if we weren't careful, we would end up like . . ."

"How did she know?" Isabel frowned.

Tía Paloma shrugged. "She guessed, and she came to me with her suspicions. Marisol has always been wary of power."

Leo wanted to feel sad. She wanted to sit down on the couch in her own house, and talk to Mamá about life and death and friendship, and what it meant that her sisters gave wrong advice, and that

Tía Paloma lied, and that magic might be more dangerous than she had ever imagined.

But she couldn't do any of that until the spirits were safe. They needed a solution.

She sat on the ground in front of the gate and dipped her arm through the veil as Isabel continued to argue. She listened to the desperation in her sister's voice. They needed a spirit who could stand on the other side of the veil and pull the spirits through. Someone—or something—who could see the gate and pass through it.

Leo could see the gate.

When her arm was inside the gate up to the shoulder, Leo bent her elbow so that her fingers poked back into the living room. With a little bit of straining, she caught one of the scraps of newspaper left behind from the dramatic opening of the portal. She held the paper between her fingers and pulled her hand into the gate once more.

The newspaper slipped through the veil, staying between her fingers as they entered the cold.

It was all the proof she needed. "I can do it," she said. "I can be the guide."

"What?" Caroline said.

"No!" said Tía Paloma.

"Don't be silly, Leo," Isabel said.

"I'm serious." She stood up and waved her arm across the gate. "I can move in and out. I'm pretty sure I can go in and pull everyone through. Easy."

"Leo," Tía Paloma said, "that's very bold of you, but you have no idea what you're offering. None of us do. A human who can pass through the veil unaccompanied and return is . . . as far as I know it's never been . . . it's completely . . ."

"Unprecedented," Caroline said.

"We have no idea what will happen if you walk through." Tía Paloma shook her head. "It's too much of a risk."

"I'll summon the guide myself," Isabel said. "Nobody else has to be involved. I can handle it."

"Reckless and foolhardy . . ." Abuela was talking fast and almost to herself. "Both of them, just like their aunt. . . ."

"This was my spell," Caroline said, "I should be the one to—"

" . . . I'll sit on them until I disintegrate if I have to. . . ."

Leo clicked her tongue in frustration. The fear, the way her sisters stared like she was offering to throw herself into a volcano or a lion's mouth, it was all wrong. She couldn't say how she knew, how she could be so certain, deep in her bones, that entering the veil wouldn't hurt her. But she was. So, to cut the argument short, to avoid wasting any more time, she crossed her arms over her chest defiantly and took one huge step backward, plunging through the veil.

Leo stumbled and fell back, landing softly in a sitting position on smooth, firm ground.

It was cold in el Otro Lado. Not cold like the weather, like freezing wind and ice, which Leo had experienced only a few times and didn't enjoy. No, this was cold like air conditioning after a long walk in the summer, like a Popsicle against your lips or an ice pack against a bruise. It was relaxation and relief, this cold that raised goose bumps on her skin but didn't pinch her bones.

She stood up and looked around. The Campbell living room surrounded her still, and everyone was still there, but they were all blurred by the shimmering layer of the veil. Either no one was speaking or she couldn't hear them. Isabel might have been crying, or maybe the wetness on her face was just the blur of the magic.

The two pillars still stood tall on either side of the gate. Leo stood, reached her hand between them, and waved.

"Leo!" Isabel clapped both hands over her mouth, her voice only a little tinny coming through the veil, like Leo was hearing it through a bad phone connection. "You are in so much trouble, you, you—you little cucaracha!"

Leo poked her head out into the living room to stick out her tongue. "I told you I could do it!"

"You are such a brat!" Isabel groaned. "You are unbelievable! You are—"

"You're kind of awesome, actually." Alma smiled. "Even Belén and I couldn't see you."

Leo reached out her hand. "Mayor Rose?" she asked. "Do you want to give your speech again?"

"No, thank you." He grinned and reached out to grip Leo's hand, just like he had shaken it at their first meeting. "Happy to follow your lead, Leo Logroño."

Leo gave his arm a tug, and he walked through the veil to join her.

"Aah . . ." The breath that rushed out of him warmed the cold air of el Otro Lado, then quickly faded. "Thank you—that's much better." He gave Leo's hand a squeeze, then let go and . . . vanished. His body dissolved like spun sugar, light bouncing in several directions before disappearing entirely.

"Mayor Rose?" Leo asked. "Mayor Rose?"

She stuck her head back through the portal. "Um, hey everyone? Alma? Belén? Tía Paloma? Does anybody see the mayor?"

"Where did he go?" Alma asked. "He was a ghost for about two seconds and then he wasn't. He's gone."

"What do you mean, gone?" Tricia gasped. "He can't be gone! What the heck is going on?"

Leo pulled her head back into el Otro Lado, but there was no sign of Mayor Rose, just the same cool quiet that had been there before. She reentered the living room, eyebrows furrowed. "Did I do something wrong?"

Abuela stepped forward and put a hand on Tía Paloma's shoulder. "I think I can explain," she said.

"Explain what?" Isabel's face looked weary and worried, her eyes still red.

"I wanted to tell you earlier, but it was just a hunch, a feeling I had." Abuela hesitated. "I had a sense that once we got back to el Otro Lado, it wouldn't be easy for us to hold ourselves together."

Having just thrown herself into a mysterious portal because of a hunch, Leo had no problem believing that Abuela was right, especially now that Mayor Rose had proven her theory correct. "But why?"

"I told you before," Abuela said. "Beyond the veil, spirits become part of everything. It takes energy to resist that pull, and we're all so drained from our time here."

"So you'll run out of energy and disintegrate?" Belén asked. "Isn't that exactly what we were trying to avoid with the spell?"

"Why did we even bother if the same thing is going to happen anyway?" Alma's voice squeaked high and angry.

"Girls." It was Mrs. Morales who spoke, one hand on Abuela's shoulder as she frowned at the twins. "Please be patient. This is hard, but I promise you—your work has not been wasted. It is not the same thing."

She explained what Leo had heard already—how losing your grip on yourself in el Otro Lado was a good thing, not a bad one. How the spirits were tired, and had spent so much energy holding themselves together in this world. They wanted to go back, and let go, and dissolve into the ocean of el Otro Lado.

"Mayor Rose was able to give up his fears and let himself go," Mrs. Morales said. "You shouldn't worry about him. If we lose ourselves here, we are alone and hollow, but there, we are whole."

"But you won't be yourself?" Alma asked, directing her question to Abuela rather than her friend. "We won't be able to talk to you?"

Abuela shook her head, eyes on the floor. "We spirits hang around the longest when we have earthly concerns to tie us here. Unfinished business, like we all had. With all of that put to rest, we'll be free, untethered. It's what happens to all spirits eventually. It's peace. Even if I wanted to fight it, I'm afraid it would take many years for me to gather my strength," Abuela said. "Maybe more years than a human life-span."

"Why didn't you tell us?" Leo demanded. She stepped out from the veil, but it felt colder in the living room, and she felt her hands shivering as she imagined Mayor Rose dissolving in front of her eyes. "You should have told me!"

Abuela left Mrs. Morales's side and wiggled in between Alma and Belén, linking arms with each girl. Leo walked to them and leaned into a tangled hug, her face twisting as she buried it in Abuela's shoulder.

"I have loved sharing this day with my granddaughters," Abuela said. "But I'm tired, and it's time for me to go."

"Will you try, at least?" Leo asked. "Will you try to hold yourself together on the other side, so we can still summon you and talk to you?"

Abuela's shoulders rose and fell with her long sigh. "The benefit of being part of everything is that

I'll always be around," she said. "You don't ever have to miss me, not really."

Tricia ran across the room to wrap Mrs. Morales in a hug. "This isn't fair," she said. "I didn't even know I could talk to you before, and now I can't do it anymore."

"You can, though," Mrs. Morales said, stroking Tricia's hair. "I'll always hear."

Isabel and Tía Paloma joined the sister group hug. Leo breathed in the smell of marigolds and herbs and candle smoke as her family warmed her cold skin.

"It isn't fair," Isabel murmuered.

"Oh, hush." Abuela shook her way out of the hug and gave Isabel a light tap on the head. "We're not suffering a tragic fate. You girls made sure of that. Now come on, Leonora. It's past time for us to go."

Leo shook her head furiously for three seconds. For three seconds she imagined she could really refuse. For three seconds she never let go of Abuela's arm, and they all went home together and ate quesadillas straight off the stove with Mamá and Daddy and everyone, and there were no boundaries.

Then the three seconds ended, and Leo broke the hug. "Okay," she said. "Who's next?"

CHAPTER 19

GOODBYES

Old Jack gave a short and confusing speech about hydrangeas before Leo pulled him through the gate, and his spirit bloomed into a ring of light before disappearing.

Leo swore she heard a tinkling melody play when Mr. Nguyen let go of her hand.

Mr. Pérez stayed solid for about fifteen seconds, and had time to adjust his leather jacket and give Leo a salute before swirling into a swarm of lights that popped like fireworks.

Mrs. Morales reminded Tricia to be good, yell at her father, and study hard. She melted softly away the instant she crossed the veil.

Finally, Leo walked arm in arm with Abuela up to the gate.

"Ready?" Leo asked. The word felt like a wad of paper on her tongue.

"Leonora Elena, you are growing up to be quite a remarkable bruja," Abuela said. "And I have to say, this birth-order power is going to be the envy of all your sisters."

"Birth-order power?" Leo asked. She looked at the veil, then back to Abuela. "Is this my . . . ?"

"Your Tía Isabel believed that all the birth-order powers derive from el Otro Lado," Abuela said. "First-borns can influence emotions by changing the energy that flows on that side of the veil. Second-borns can tap into the energy to manifest physical objects just like these cempazuchitl petals. Third-borns see beyond the veil, of course. And you, Leo, seem to be capable of passing through it."

"I'm actually not that envious," Belén said, smiling through watery eyes.

"But we needed a whole portal spell for me to do this," Leo said. "Don't most birth-order powers happen a little more easily?"

"You're so young," Tía Paloma said. "It's conceivable that the power might grow stronger as you come of age. I'm not sure what that means for you, what exactly you'll be able to do, but it's certainly going to be interesting to watch. Oh, your mother will be so proud."

Abuela's black-hole eyes twinkled as she tugged Leo's elbow. "Enough talk, Leonora. Pull me through and put this old hag to rest already, before we all die of old age."

Leo stepped through into the cold blurry version of the living room, reached her hand out, closed her eyes, and pulled.

"Goodbye," she whispered as the weight of Abuela's hand in hers grew lighter, less substantial, until it was nothing at all.

"That's it," Caroline said. "It's over." Her eyes were red, and she sat on the carpet with her legs splayed in front of her like she might never move again.

Leo wanted to join her. Her heart hurt even as it glowed with pride in her friends, her family, herself. They had done it.

It should have felt better.

Unfortunately, she couldn't lie on the floor just yet.

"Caroline?" she asked. "When does your dad get home?"

"Oh." Caroline stared around the room, a disaster of crumpled newspaper, candle wax, and interesting spells. "It's kind of a mess, isn't it?"

It is, Leo thought, *and she can't even see the towering glowing gate to the afterlife in the middle of the room.*

"I can help clean," Brent said.

"We can do it," Mai chimed in. "Don't worry, Caroline, you can rest."

Tricia nodded.

Just for this one second, Leo wished her friends weren't so helpful. How was she supposed to distract Caroline if they offered to do everything for her?

"Maybe you should make some tea," Leo tried.

"That's a great idea," Tía Paloma agreed. "Come on, Caroline, I've got you." She held out a hand and hoisted the young bruja to her feet. "What kind of tea, love?"

Leo watched as they disappeared into the kitchen. "Okay," she whispered, glancing around the room. "Now's our chance."

"Huh?" Brent asked too loudly. Leo glared her hardest glare (*Abuela, help me look as scary as you,* she thought). She stood in front of the gate.

"Come on, hurry."

Mrs. Campbell wiggled out from under the couch.

Tricia, who had understood the glare better than Brent, clapped her hand over his mouth when he opened it to yell. She and Mai stared wide-eyed at Leo, who nodded.

"Please don't tell," she whispered.

"Explain later?" Belén asked, watching Mrs. Campbell free herself from her hiding spot with curiosity.

"I promise," Leo said.

"Sorry if I alarmed you all," Mrs. Campbell whispered, brushing herself off and walking to Leo. "I used to be pretty good at hide-and-seek, if I do say so myself."

Leo tried to smile, but the edges of her mouth felt too weary. "Ready?" she asked for the seventh time, holding out her hand even though she didn't feel ready herself. There were too many goodbyes.

"Quick," Mrs. Campbell said softly.

So Leo went quick, pulling Caroline's mother into el Otro Lado.

Like Mr. Pérez, Mrs. Campbell stayed solid at first, her hand keeping its shape even as Leo dropped it and turned around.

"Thank you," Mrs. Campbell said, "for all your help."

"Are you sure you want to go?" Leo asked, even

though it might already be too late. "Are you positive you wouldn't rather see Caroline? And let her see you one more time?" It hurt that Abuela was gone, that this separation would be more final. But Leo wouldn't trade it. She had spent the day with her grandmother, and that was good no matter what happened next.

Mrs. Campbell sighed. "One of the very few upsides to a long cancer battle"—she smiled wryly—"is that you get plenty of time to say goodbye. You can plan, and write letters, record videos. There was nothing much I could say that I haven't said already. But there was something I needed to do."

"Your unfinished business," Leo said, "What was it?"

"I didn't plan it," Mrs. Campbell said. "And I certainly didn't expect it to turn out quite like this. But when I watched Caroline visit Costa Rica, and then come back here—she felt out of place, she felt so alone. And . . . oh dear." Mrs. Campbell's legs had started to bubble and fizz like the top of a poured soda. "I wished for a way to show her that she wasn't alone, with or without me. That her Costa Rican heritage isn't lost, and her Tica family will always be part of her. That she has friends. Like Brent, and Tricia, and Mai, and especially you. That she is connected to so many people in so many ways." She was nothing but light and dust particles from the waist down, and the tips of her fingers had started to fizz. "I hope she knows that now."

"She does," Leo said into the empty space where Mrs. Campbell no longer stood. "I'll make sure she does."

"What were you doing in there, Leo?" Caroline was in the living room, mug of tea in one hand and a mini vacuum cleaner in the other. Isabel, Tía Paloma, and the twins all stood between her and the gate, but they had failed to block her view of Leo's reappearance.

"Oh, just . . . experimenting," Leo said.

"I can't believe you have enough energy for that." Caroline laughed. "I feel like I'd be okay with a twelve-hour nap, and you're off doing magical experiments. So what's it like over there?"

Leo hesitated, trying to come up with something to tell her friend. "Um. It's cool?"

There was a soft pop and a light breeze, and the light behind Leo faded. When she turned around, the light columns were collapsing down and in, their colorful foundation winding like thread on a spool back into the opening that shrank and shrank and then was gone. There was a final puff of petals, all colors, that fell to the floor.

"Oh wow," Caroline said. "You must've done something."

Leo nodded slowly. "I guess so," she said, not wanting to tell Caroline that the spell had ended as soon as all the spirits were delivered across the gate.

Caroline came closer, holding out the mug. "I made you one," she said. "You said your sisters get tired after using their powers."

Leo beamed and accepted the tea. "Chamomile," she said as she inhaled the steam. "For relaxing."

"And cinnamon for strength." Caroline nodded. "Your aunt said she would start teaching me, but I already have most of the herbs memorized from helping you. Aren't you excited? We get to learn about magic together!"

Leo nodded. "It's going to be double the awesome," she agreed. "But you know we would have anyway, even if you didn't have any powers."

"I know," Caroline said. "Besides, I'm not just another Logroño girl. I have my own family traditions to learn about. I was texting my prima, and she said she'd dig around my grandma's old stuff, to try to find any spells or magical items. And when I go back for spring break, we can go visit my grandma's cousin and see if she knows anything. I can't wait."

Warmth bubbled in Leo's chest. Mrs. Campbell didn't have anything to worry about.

"Leo, don't cry," Caroline said. "I'm sorry; I'm being terrible, acting excited when your grandma just . . . when you had to say goodbye."

"No, don't worry," Leo said. "I'm happy, really. For Abuela and all the spirits. They're safe and peaceful. I think I'm just tired, like you said." Caroline squeezed her shoulder, and Leo sipped a mouthful of warm tea.

"Hey, what's this?" Alma asked. She stood over the spot where the portal had vanished, staring at the colorful petals that had replaced it. "It almost looks like an ofrenda."

The purple, green, yellow, red, and blue petals had formed shapes among the orange to form a rectangle of intricate designs, with a sunburst circle pattern overlapping its lower half. Leo had seen flower petals formed into pictures as part of the ofrenda displays for Día de los Muertos, but those were usually in the shapes of skulls or crosses. This shape had a thin line sticking off one end, almost making it look like some kind of wheelbarrow or wagon, but nothing she recognized.

"A gate?" Mai guessed. She tilted her head to one side. "Or a flag?"

"No, it's like a chariot," Brent said. "See the wheel?"

"He's right, but it isn't a chariot wheel." Caroline said. "It's a carreta."

Leo glanced at Isabel. "A cart?" her sister translated uncertainly.

"Yeah, an oxcart. You know, one of the little painted ones?" Caroline pointed to the circular designs. "My grandma has pictures of them. They're traditional in Costa Rica. I think she used to decorate them for festivals."

"Huh?" Leo still didn't know what her friend was talking about.

"Don't worry about it," Caroline said. A tiny smile formed on her face. "It's a Tica thing. And it's one more thing for me to vacuum before my dad gets back."

With that, everyone got to cleaning. But in spite of what Caroline had said, she carefully vacuumed around the edges of the design, leaving it undisturbed for as long as possible.

Everyone else was bustling, tidying up the kitchen or loading trash into bags to haul to the bakery (so

Mr. Campbell wouldn't wonder why his garbage can smelled like a botánica).

"What else can I do to help?" Leo asked as Caroline changed the vacuum attachment to clean under the chairs.

"Hey," she said. She knelt down, reached her hand under the couch, and withdrew something small and shiny.

"What is it?" Leo asked, a little nervous. Had Mrs. Campbell left some evidence of her hiding? How would Caroline feel if she found out the truth now?

Caroline held up a silver ring with a tiny butterfly topping it, its orange wings webbed with thin black lines. "I know what this is. I got it on a trip to Costa Rica when I was little, but I lost it years ago." She looked down at the floor. "And I'm pretty sure we've moved the couch since then. . . ."

"Wow, that's really cool; it's so pretty," Leo said, trying to distract Caroline's train of thought. "The wings look like the petals from the spirits, a little."

"Leo . . . can I ask you something, even if it sounds silly?"

"Mmhm?"

"Do you think maybe . . . even if my mom didn't have unfinished business, even if she didn't get pulled through by my spell . . . do you think she could have been watching anyway? I just felt like there was something there. Something helping me today."

"I think that makes sense," Leo said. "Abuela said that in el Otro Lado, you can be part of everything, all at once. So I think she probably was part of what happened."

Caroline smiled. She slipped the ring onto her finger. "I'm really sorry about your grandma, Leo."

"I'm really sorry about your mom." As Leo said it, she realized that she wasn't sure she had ever said it to Caroline before.

"All right," Caroline said, giving herself a shake. "We should definitely keep cleaning, unless you want to explain all this bruja stuff to my dad today, because I know I don't. I'll save that for after I know a little more about it myself!"

Leo nodded. "That will probably be soon, though. Something tells me you're going to learn fast."

CHAPTER 20
EVERYWHERE

It was dark outside when Leo woke up. The moon showed silver through her blinds and her alarm clock read 4:01, and she should have been sleeping still. There was nothing to wake her, not a hand or a voice or the loud laugh that had been playing in her dream. She rubbed her eyes and sat up with none of her usual reluctance.

It was January 6, Día de los Reyes, and Leo tip-toed into the kitchen in her socks and fuzzy pajama pants, because there was something she needed to do.

Alma and Belén joined her just as she finished gathering the ingredients, ready to slice the oranges.

Isabel arrived in time to heat the sugar sauce in a pot on the stove. Marisol shuffled in much later, after the boiling and freezing (and boiling again) was all finished, but she helped roll the drying pieces in their final coat of sugar.

"Girls?" Mamá entered the kitchen with a sweat-shirt pulled over her long nightgown. "What are you doing up?"

Leo held out one of the plates of candied orange slices, the plate Isabel had decorated by overlapping the bright half circles to look like the crowded petals of a giant blooming marigold.

"Happy Kings' Day, Mamá."

"You girls." Mamá smiled. She chose her slice carefully between two fingers and closed her eyes as she chewed. "Did you plan this?"

Leo looked at Isabel, who looked at the twins, who looked at Marisol, who shrugged and ate two more slices off her bare-looking plate. "Not really," she said, spraying grains of sugar from her mouth.

Daddy entered the kitchen, putting his hands on Mamá's shoulders and letting her feed him a slice of sweet orange. "Not bad," he said in his grumbly waking-up voice. "What recipe did you use?"

Leo shrugged along with her sisters. "It's just equal parts water and sugar," Isabel said.

"With a splash of orange juice," Alma added.

"We were just . . ." Marisol shrugged. "Inspired."

"By the holiday," Belén said.

Mamá lined up the five plates of slices on the counter, a smile on her face even as she blinked quickly and cleared her throat. "I always liked to do full circles, myself. Or just the peel for decorating. It was your grandmother who made them this way."

Leo wasn't exactly surprised, but hearing the words out loud popped the dreamlike bubble she had been working in, and everything that had felt clear and simple since she woke up twisted with mystery and longing.

"I stopped using them on our rosca de reyes," Mamá said. "They're a little too bitter for some people, and there are so many festive alternatives."

"We could make a special cake with them," Isabel said. "We could eat it tonight! Oh, and we should invite Caroline and her dad."

"That sounds nice," Daddy said. "I like Mr. Campbell."

"We should invite Leo's other friends too," Alma said, "since they helped with everything too. And I think we technically owe that one boy cake."

"Wait, if Leo's friends are all coming over, then

I want to invite my boyf—my, um friend," Marisol said.

"Why not?" Mamá laughed. "Let's throw a whole party, at the last minute, on a day when I'm working and the kitchen is a mess."

"Oh, Elena." Daddy hugged Mamá from behind. "Where's your holiday spirit?"

"I didn't say no," Mamá said, a smile tweaking the edges of her mouth. "Invite the whole town if you want. I'm just not going to be the one organizing."

"Good, because I already texted him." Marisol smiled sweetly, phone in hand.

"Don't touch those dishes," Daddy said, barring Mamá's way as she headed for the sink. "Leave all that to me. I'll get this place party ready in no time. What time does the dollar store open, do you think?"

Mamá rolled her eyes, but she smiled, put an arm around Leo's shoulders, and squeezed. "How did I get such a great family?" she asked as Isabel dug out a clean frying pan and a carton of eggs to start real breakfast.

Leo smiled. "Well, you do have magic bruja powers. That probably helps."

"Hey," Daddy protested. "I've been hearing a lot of chatter and gossip about nonbruja and brujo folks, and I just want to point out that you girls have one nonmagical parent who's *right here* if you have any questions about whether nonmagical people can be trusted with secrets. I happen to think that I've done a pretty good job of integrating into your mother's world."

"Sorry, Daddy," Isabel said sheepishly. "I wasn't thinking about you when I told Leo all that. You don't really count."

"Yeah," Leo pointed out. "Anyway, Abuela told me last year that everyone has some kind of magic. It just might not be as obvious as ours. Even your family."

"Well, if that's true, it's news to me." Daddy shrugged. "Until Elena told me, I thought brujería was all rumor and superstition. I was sure that I could explain everything in the world with plain facts and logic. But then I learned better."

"That sounds like how Mario responded when I told him." Marisol giggled.

"Wait, Mario?" Daddy asked. "Is that the name of the boy we're going to meet? What happened to George?"

"Daddyyyy," Marisol groaned. "That was weeks ago."

Next to Leo, Mamá squinted down at the counter, then plucked a small marigold blossom from nowhere and settled it in the corner of Isabel's plate.

"I'd better get dressed for work," she said. "But leave at least seven, will you? Just in case our guests from yesterday can enjoy them."

Leo remembered Abuela's words. The benefit of being everything . . .

When she looked at Mamá's flower, she thought she could see a layer of something shimmering over it.

"They can," she said. "They already do."

When no one was looking, she reached for the flower and felt the chill of cool air against her fingertips as they disappeared.

EPILOGUE

APRIL VISITOR

Leo's body twitched violently, startled out of a dream that smelled like marigolds and left goose bumps on her skin. A good dream, but not a good feeling holding her muscles tensed now. Something moved in her room.

Slowly she opened one eye, scanning the bedside table, the bookshelves and the dollhouse in front of the window, the corner where her closet door stood open with its crooked line of hangers. Everything seemed undisturbed. She shifted as naturally as she could to check the foot of her bed.

Nothing. Just a feeling, or a nightmare. She sat

up in bed and hugged her knees to her chest to calm her beating heart.

In the empty space where she had been staring, a dark figure appeared.

"Gah!" Leo kicked her legs and lifted her hands to her face and thought about screaming for real to bring Mamá and Daddy running. But a thought occurred to her. "Abuela?"

"Afraid not," an unfamiliar voice replied. It was deep and friendly, but it did nothing to relax Leo's clenched fists.

"Who are you?" she demanded. "What are you doing here?" It was midnight by the alarm clock on her bedside table. "What do you want?"

The figure stepped to the side of the bed, moving slowly, hands raised to show innocence. Leo made out a wrinkled brown face and a tall shock of gray hair, combed to one side. The man—or spirit—was smiling. "I just want to talk," he said.

"Well, I don't talk to strangers," Leo replied, just about making up her mind to scream.

"Now, now, Leo. Is that any way to treat your abuelo Logroño?"

LEOÑORA'S

LUCKY RECIPE BOOK #2

ROSCA DE REYES: "THREE KINGS' CAKE"

Makes one cake. Be careful where you bite . . . there may be a tiny baby inside your slice.

INGREDIENTS

FOR DOUGH

½ stick unsalted butter, plus more for greasing the baking tray
1 cup granulated sugar
4 eggs
½ cup milk
½ teaspoon salt
2½ cups flour
2 tablespoons yeast (activated in warm milk)
1 cup lard (optional)
2 small ceramic baby Jesus figures (NOT PLASTIC!*)

FOR TOPPING

1½ cups flour
1 stick butter
½ cup icing sugar

½ cup granulated sugar

2 cups dried and candied fruit

DIRECTIONS FOR DOUGH

In a large mixing bowl, combine the ½ stick of butter and sugar and mix for four minutes. Add the eggs, one at a time, mixing throughout, and then the milk and salt for 1 minute.

Add the flour and the yeast that's been activated in warm milk and mix for 3 minutes.

Add the optional lard and mix 8 minutes until the mixture isn't sticking to the bowl.

Cover the dough loosely with plastic wrap or a cloth; let it sit and rise until it's doubled in size. This will take approximately 1 to 1½ hours.

Put the mixing bowl in the refrigerator and let the risen dough rest for another 30 minutes.

Put the dough onto a lightly floured board. Roll and shape the dough into a donut-like rosca de reyes.

Grease your baking tray with the unsalted butter. Lay the dough ring on the tray and let it rest uncovered for another 30 minutes.

Preheat the oven to 350 degrees.

Make the topping (see next page).

Spread the topping over the dough. Insert each of the ceramic babies into the bottom of the cake in a different spot so that they are hidden from view.

Bake the cake for 30 minutes.

Once the cake is cool, add the dried and candied fruit to the top.

DIRECTIONS FOR THE TOPPING:

Combine the flour, butter, icing sugar, and granulated sugar and mix for 7 minutes or until you get a paste that's the texture of butter.

You will put the dried and candied fruit on the cake once it is baked.

*Plastic babies may be hidden in a baked and cooled cake by pushing them in from the bottom.

HOT CHOCOLATE

Makes four servings.

INGREDIENTS

3 tablespoons crushed cinnamon sticks
3 cups whole milk
6 ounces semisweet chocolate, chopped
3 tablespoons granulated sugar
¾ teaspoon vanilla extract or almond extract
pinch of salt
¼ teaspoon ground cayenne pepper, plus more for topping if desired
whipped cream
cocoa powder

DIRECTIONS

In a saucepan over medium-low heat, bring cinnamon and milk to a simmer. Make sure to whisk so the milk does not boil until you can smell the cinnamon. It should take about 10 minutes.

Whisk in the chocolate, sugar, vanilla or almond extract, salt, and ¼ teaspoon of cayenne. Make sure to whisk frequently until the mixture is smooth and the chocolate is fully melted and creamy. Should take about 6 minutes.

Remove from heat. Set out four mugs. Divide the hot chocolate among the mugs. Add whipped cream to the top and sprinkle it with cocoa powder and more cayenne pepper if you desire.

ACKNOWLEDGMENTS

In this book, Leo and her sisters learn that you can never have too many witches in the kitchen. Just like a multilayered spell, publication depends on a community of talented individuals working together. I extend my deepest thanks to everyone who has added their love and magic to this book, including but definitely not limited to:

Dhonielle Clayton and Sona Charaipotra, Cake Literary partners extraordinaire, for giving the first spark of life to Leo and her stories.

Jordan Brown for his tireless work to make this book the best it could possibly be, and Debbie Kovacs for her industry expertise.

Victoria Marini for her continued support as I navigate all the facets of my writing career.

Mirelle Ortega for once again blowing me away with perfect cover art, and Jessie Gang and Sarah

Nichole Kaufman for the logo and jacket design. The books are so beautiful it actually makes me cry.

Everyone at Walden Pond Press and HarperCollins for all the time, effort, and faith in this story.

My parents and my brothers for supporting me and letting me talk about obscure book stuff. All my family for promoting the heck out of book one, cheering me on through book two, and offering all sorts of suggestions for books three through one hundred. I love and appreciate all of you (though I can't promise that fart magic is ever going to make it into the series).

All my friends for being gracious whenever I fall off the grid for promotion and deadline stuff. The New School squad for absolutely crushing it and sharing all the best advice and motivation. Andrea, Devon and Claire, and Brandon for emergency Spanish questions, Costa Rica consultations, and naming debates. Mary for listening to me ramble-outline the original plot. Ariel for beta reading, copyediting, and letting me ride on the back of your bike.

My writing people, teacher friends, booksellers and librarians, students, and everyone who has enjoyed reading about Leo. I really can't express how much it means.

Thank y'all so much.

Turn the page for a sneak peek at

LOVE SUGAR MAGIC:
A MIXTURE OF MISCHIEF

CHAPTER 1

SO MUCH TO LEARN

Amor y Azúcar Panadería had closed its doors for the night, but inside the warm kitchen, Leo Logroño's work was just beginning.

"I'm ready, Mamá," she said, setting down her knife and wiping her hands on her apron, leaving dark wet streaks amid the generous dusting of flour.

Leo's mother perched on a stool in the corner near the large bakery ovens. She appeared to be focused on the day's receipts, but Leo could see that her mother's eyes were following her every move. "Don't tell me about it," she said, waving a hand toward the oven and lifting her papers closer to her face to hide her smile. "This is your *independent* baking test."

Leo took a deep breath and nodded. She lifted her tray carefully, forcing her eyes off her six oblong dough loaves so she could watch her step. Should she have made the loaves smaller? Had she given them enough time to rise so their insides would be light and fluffy? Her dough looked all right, and the tiny piece she'd snuck into her mouth, once she'd finished mixing and kneading it, tasted all right—much better than the first time she had tried to make this recipe from memory.

But still, Leo wondered if it would be enough to pass Mamá's standards. She slid her tray into the oven, set the timer and steamer for ideal crusty loaves, and breathed a small sigh of relief. If nothing else, she'd gotten this batch into the oven without dropping it, unlike the last one.

Leo had spent weeks pestering Mamá to let her take on more work in the bakery, to give her a job in the kitchen with her older sisters instead of always sticking her behind the cash register. That's how they had come to their current agreement: If Leo could bake a batch of the bakery's basic bread loaf from memory, all by herself, then Mamá would put her on rotation to work in the kitchen. This was

Leo's third attempt, not counting one disastrous kneading session in the kitchen at home. She had started today's dough just before the bakery closed, letting it rise while she helped her sisters clean and close up shop. The wait had made her hopes rise too, and now she felt ready to burst with anticipation.

"How do they look?" she asked, bouncing a little on the balls of her feet.

"We'll have to see when they come out," Mamá said, but her eyes twinkled, and Leo's chest loosened. She climbed onto the second stool next to Mamá and let out a tired puff of breath, wiping wild tendrils of escaped hair off her forehead and back under her baseball cap. Sometimes her older sisters got away with tight ponytails and buns in the bakery, but Leo's hair needed extra containment.

"You know, if you start working during business hours you won't get much of a break," Mamá reminded her. "There's always a batch to take out of the oven, or a new one to start mixing, or—"

"I know!" Leo laughed. "But since I won't have you watching me and making me nervous, I won't need a break."

Mamá clicked her tongue. "I don't know what you're talking about. I've just been going over the books." She conjured a mechanical pencil out of thin air and made a note in the margins of the paper in front of her just to prove her point.

Leo copied Mamá's hand motion, a pinch of her fingers and a flick of her wrist, imagining that she too had the bruja power of manifestation. Second-born daughters in the family—like Mamá, and like Leo's sixteen-year-old sister, Marisol—could make small objects appear and disappear as easily as first-borns could manipulate emotions and third-borns could communicate with spirits from el Otro Lado.

As the fourth-born daughter, the first of her kind in generations of Rose Hill brujas, Leo didn't yet know exactly what her special power would be, though she suspected it might have something to do with her ability to see the veil between this world and el Otro Lado. She had discovered that power in January, when her friend Caroline had accidentally thrown open a gate between the world of the living and the world of the dead.

The problem was, being able to see the veil wasn't the most exciting kind of power. Sometimes, if Leo concentrated really hard, she could find the shadowy shimmery veil and poke her fingers through it, but it wasn't nearly as useful a power as making objects from nothing.

"I know I can be a real baker," Leo said, eyes on the oven door. Everyone else helped in the kitchen, even Marisol, who hated spending time away from her friends, and Alma and Belén, who were still in ninth grade. Just because she was young didn't mean she couldn't do the same. Mamá was giving Leo a chance to prove that she was old enough to take on more responsibility. It was the chance Leo had been waiting for. She just hadn't realized it would be so scary.

Mamá reached across the gap between the stools to give Leo's shoulder a squeeze. "Always in such a hurry to grow up," she said. Then she jumped to her feet. "Well, come on. We've left a mess, and real bakers clean up after themselves."

By the time Leo had wiped her work space, washed and dried all her dishes, and returned everything to its proper place, the air was thick with its normal daytime smell of warm yeast and flour. She paced in front of the glass oven door as her timer ticked down, peeking in at the lonely looking tray in the big empty belly of the oven. She let out a squeal of excitement when she finally pulled out the tray and saw six beautiful golden bolillos, the crusty bread that made for a perfect side dish as well as the very best sandwiches.

"They look wonderful," Mamá confirmed, and she picked up one of the small hot loaves with her bare hand, something Leo would have gotten in trouble for. "Ready to try it?" She ripped the bolillo in half and offered one steaming end to Leo. On Mamá's nod, Leo bit into her piece, teeth crunching through the outside and sinking into the soft middle. Buttery, fresh, and hot, the bolillo tasted like victory on her tongue.

"Well," Mamá said, chewing thoughtfully, "I'd be a fool to argue with that. Consider yourself eligible for back-of-the-house shifts. You can start tomorrow morning if you like."

Leo leaped into the air, bread raised in triumph. Tomorrow was Saturday, which meant she had two full weekend days to practice working alongside her sisters. She was going to be an expert baker in no time!

Mamá held up a warning finger. "You'll start off slow. Bolillos only for now, and just a couple of batches at a time." Her face stayed stern for three seconds before softening. "Good job, 'jita."

"Thank you." Leo couldn't wait to get home and tell her sisters. Isabel would be proud like Mamá, and Alma and Belén would claim not to be surprised. Marisol might pretend to wonder why anyone would celebrate having more work to do, but she'd probably be happy to swap baking for Leo's shifts at the register in the front of the bakery. Leo nibbled her bread while Mamá shut down the oven for the night, her heart glowing like the fading light of the oven heating coils.

But after her third bite, her jubilation faded. Something tasted . . . off.

"Let's bring these home," Mamá said, packing Leo's loaves into a paper bag and rinsing the tray in the oversized sink. "I've been craving capirotada now that it's almost Easter, and these would be perfect for it."

Leo took the bag Mamá offered her with a frown. "Are you sure?" she asked. "Are you positive I got the recipe right?"

"Sure I'm sure," Mamá scanned the kitchen one last time. "Why, what's wrong?"

Leo shrugged. She bit off another piece of the bread. It tasted good, and it tasted like a bolillo, but something was . . . different. It didn't taste like an Amor y Azúcar bolillo. It was like when Mamá bought store-brand cereal—similar, but not quite the same.

"They don't seem exactly right," Leo said. "Should I try again tomorrow night? Maybe I added too much flour and dried out the dough. . . ." She pulled a tiny spiral notebook out of her back pocket, flipping through the pages to see her notes on this batch.

"Wait, 'jita, slow down. You did great," Mamá said. "Is this about nerves? You don't have to start work tomorrow if you don't want to. I know it can be a lot of pressure, but nobody expects you to keep up with everything your older sisters do."

"It's not nerves." Leo shook her head, disappointment weighing down the corners of her mouth. "I want to work in the bakery. I want to be a real baker. But I must have done something wrong. This bolillo doesn't taste like yours."

To her surprise, Mamá laughed. "Well, of course it doesn't. I thought it would be cheating to let you use the mixing bowl."

"The mixing bowl?" Leo knew which bowl Mamá meant—the extra-large wooden one in which Marisol or the twins usually prepared the oversized batches of bolillo dough. Leo had always assumed the bowl was used for its size, not as part of the recipe.

"Indeed," Mamá said, opening one of the tall wooden cabinets and taking out the mixing bowl. "I know that the baking equipment we use doesn't usually make a difference. But this is a family heirloom. There's power in something passed down through the generations."

"Power to make bread tasty?" Leo asked, running

her hand down the smooth side of the bowl. She breathed deep and caught a whiff of her family's spicy magic scent.

Mamá nodded. "Power to make recipes turn out better than perfect."

"So it's another type of relic," Leo said. Tía Paloma, Mamá's younger sister who helped in the bakery and with the magical education of Leo and her sisters, had taught her about objects that could be used to strengthen and channel magic. She just hadn't mentioned that they used a relic to make the daily batches of bread.

"Exactly right." Mamá flipped the lights off, leaving the closed kitchen in darkness except for the dim office light by the back door.

"Why didn't you tell me?"

"It never came up," Mamá said. "It's not like you needed to know it for your baking test."

Leo sighed. As far as Mamá was concerned, Leo never *needed to know* anything.

"You're taking to your lessons well, Paloma says. And your baking has improved so much. You have nothing to worry about, 'jita. Now come on." Mamá held out her hand for Leo to take. "Let's get to bed. We have work in the morning."

* * *

They were most of the way home, and Leo was watching the crescent moon follow them through the streets of Rose Hill when a question popped into her mind.

"Mamá? When I've finished memorizing normal bakery recipes, will I have to memorize all the recipes in the spell book too?" The idea was exciting, but daunting. The family spell book was an heirloom as old as the mixing bowl, and each bruja in the family added new magical recipes to the ever-growing compendium.

"Oh no!" Mamá raised her eyebrows and laughed. "The uses of some of the items in the book are so rare, there's no point in knowing them all by heart. That's part of the reason we write them down, so the knowledge doesn't get lost even if it's used infrequently. After you master the basic recipes and spells we use in everyday baking, I might start you on learning spice magic, at least until we figure out what your birth-order power is and whether it requires special training."

"Spice magic?" Leo asked. "But I already learned the spices and herbs. Tía Paloma quizzed me on all their uses."

Mamá turned onto their block and into the Logroño driveway. "Those are the fundamentals, the properties that brujas and brujos of any discipline should know. I'm talking about studying the specific applications of spices in baking spells—the secrets of any family of brujas cocineras."

Leo's heart beat faster—the same as it did anytime she learned about a family secret. "When can I start?"

Mamá's laugh broke the quiet of the stilled engine. "Let's work on making you a 'real baker' first, 'jita. I know you're in a hurry to learn everything at once, but I promise you, there's no rush."

Leo jumped out of the car, barely hearing Mamá's words. She slammed the car door behind her, head already scheming. Starting first thing tomorrow, she would prove she had mastered baking as soon as possible. Then Mamá would have to let her learn all the secrets of spice magic.

Mamá didn't understand how it felt, how Leo always got held back while her older sisters moved ahead. Leo didn't want to be the extra tagalong sister, the unnecessary fourth-born who didn't even have a birth-order power. She wanted to be a bruja, and a baker, and an important part of her family.

She clutched her paper bag of near-perfect bolillos to her chest. This was a good step in the right direction, but she had much more work to do.

More Must-Read Books from Walden Pond Press

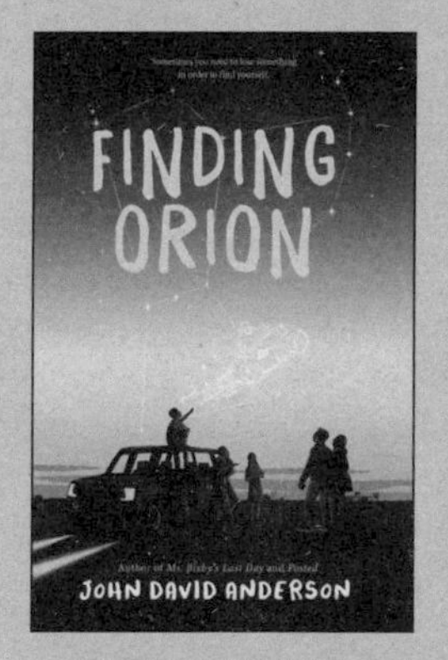

Also available as ebooks.

www.walden.com/books • www.harpercollinschildrens.com